WHISPERS OF Willow Creek

By Grace Zach

INDIA • SINGAPORE • MALAYSIA

DISCLAIMER

This is a work of fiction. Names, characters, places, businesses, events, and incidents are either the product of the author's imagination or used in a fictitious manner. Any resemblance to actual persons, living or dead, or actual events is purely coincidental.

The novel explores themes of personal growth, emotional struggles, and healing, and while it may depict moments of hardship, heartbreak, and recovery, it is intended purely for storytelling purposes. The settings, including Ronks, Lancaster County, Pennsylvania, and Chicago, Illinois, are used for atmospheric and fictional purposes and may not accurately reflect their real-world counterparts.

This book is not intended to provide psychological, financial, or career advice. Any decisions inspired by the characters or events in this novel should be made with personal discretion.

CONTENTS

EPILOGUE

Sophia Carter, a powerhouse in the world of finance and a self-made billionaire in the heart of New York, seemed to have everything: success, wealth, and influence. But beneath the dazzling facade lay a woman weighed down by loneliness, exhaustion, and a life that no longer felt like her own. Desperate to escape the relentless grind, she makes an impulsive decision to return to the one place that ever felt like home: Willow Creek, the serene countryside town where she spent her childhood summers. What she didn't expect was to run into Ethan Walker, the boy she once knew, now a man whose simple, grounded life is everything she never realized she needed. As old memories resurface and unexpected sparks fly, Sophia begins to question whether true happiness was ever in the city or if it had been waiting for her in the serenity of Willow Creek all along.

CHAPTER 1: THE VEIL

The storm had rolled in early that evening, spreading darkness all around and blurring the view into mild rainy smoke, wild and untamed, like it conveyed secrets from the sky. Rain lashed against the windows in relentless bursts, and the wind murmured like it was trying to sneak in through the cracks of the little wooden cottage nestled on the edge of Willow Creek. The fireplace cracked softly, emitting gleams of golden light that danced along the walls, but even the gentle warmth couldn't drive away the chill that crept through the air.

Sophia Carter, barely seven years old, sat on the faded corduroy armchair in the living room, her knees tucked beneath her chin and her small arms wrapped tightly around her teddy bear , a floppy, stitched-up creature with one eye missing and patches sewn on lovingly by her grandmother. Its stuffing had grown lumpy with time, but it was her constant companion, her source of quiet comfort in a world that often didn't make much sense.

The room smelled like rain-damp wool and the lemon polish her grandmother used on the wooden floors. Somewhere in the kitchen, the old kettle was beginning to whistle, but even that soft sound couldn't distract her from the strange tension that had taken over the house that evening. Her grandparents had been quieter than usual. Her grandfather, a towering man with snow-white hair and a voice like gravel, hadn't cracked a joke all day. And her grandmother, always humming while she worked, hadn't uttered a single tune.

Sophia didn't know what was wrong. She only knew that something was.

Then it happened.

A bang at the door, so loud, so abrupt, that it sliced through the silence like lightning through the sky.

Sophia jumped, the bear slipping from her arms and tumbling to the floor. Her wide eyes darted toward the front door, the sound still reverberating in her tiny chest like an aftershock. For a moment, no one moved.

Then her grandfather rose.

He didn't hurry. He moved with that slow, deliberate caution he reserved for broken things and unfamiliar animals. She could see the stiffness in his shoulders as he approached the door, pausing for a fraction of a second before unlatching it.

The door creaked open. A gust of wind howled into the room, trailing leaves and the scent of wet soil. And then entered a man.

He stumbled through the doorway like he'd been running for miles. His boots dragged muddy streaks across the floorboards, and his coat, soaked through, clung to him like a second skin. Sophia's eyes locked onto his hands first. They were smeared in something dark, something that looked too thick to be just water.

Blood.

The man's face was pale, his eyes frantic as if trying to make sense of where he was. He looked around wildly before dropping to his knees right there in the entryway.

"I… I couldn't save him," he gasped, clutching the sides of his head like the weight of the world had just come crashing down. His voice cracked under the force of his grief. "I tried. God, I tried…"

Sophia didn't understand.

She didn't know who this man was or why he looked like he'd stepped out of a nightmare. But the way her grandmother gasped, a sharp, wounded sound, sent shivers down Sophia's spine. The older woman's hand flew to her chest, her face crumbling as she turned toward her granddaughter.

"Sophia," she said, her voice thin and trembling, "go to the kitchen. Now."

The little girl hesitated, her legs glued to the chair, but her grandmother was already rushing to her, guiding her small frame behind the kitchen counter, shielding her as if hiding her from something poisonous.

"Don't come out until I tell you," her grandmother whispered. "No matter what you hear."

Sophia nodded, biting her lower lip. Her heart pounded so hard she thought it might burst out of her ribs. As soon as her grandmother turned back to the living room, Sophia peeked through the narrow space between the cabinets, curiosity clawing at her like tiny, invisible hands.

The man was still on the floor, still soaked and shaking. His hair hung over his face in wet strands, and the blood on his hands now stained the floor. He kept muttering to himself. Apologies. Pleas. Prayers.

Her grandfather stood frozen a few feet away, his knuckles white where he clutched the back of a chair. His mouth was open, forming words he couldn't say.

Then came the words that didn't feel real.

"His wife is in the hospital," the man whispered.

Sophia's grandmother's breath hitched, her shoulders stiffening.

"But he… he didn't make it."

Silence.

The kind that roars louder than any scream.

Sophia saw her grandmother stumble back like someone had punched her, her hands still hovering near her chest, her face portrayed disbelief. Her grandfather collapsed into a chair as if his knees could no longer carry him, his strong hands now trembling.

"No," he whispered. "No, no, no…"

The stranger on the floor began sobbing again, louder this time, rocking back and forth, his anguish reverberating off the walls like a haunted melody.

Sophia couldn't process it all, but even at her young age, she felt it; something was gone. Something important. Something irreplaceable. She didn't know what death really meant. But she knew her father wasn't coming home.

Ever.

She crouched lower, hugging her bear close again, trying to make herself small enough to disappear. She watched as the grown-ups dissolved into chaos, grief folding them in like a violent tide. It wasn't just the storm outside that was terrifying anymore, it was the storm inside the house.

Outside, the rain intensified, hammering the roof with a vengeance. The thunder cracked like angry gods arguing in the sky, but none of it mattered. The real thunder was in that living room, inside her grandparents' cries and the stranger's sobs, inside the sound of something breaking that could never be put back together.

Sophia didn't cry. Not yet.

She stayed behind the counter, clutching her bear so hard the seams dug into her fingers. She kept watching until the voices blurred and the shapes in the room lost their edges. She waited for someone to come get her. To hold her. To say something that would make sense of it all.

But no one came. No one had answers.

Complete silence prevailed over the chaos, the kind of silence that swallowed everything. The only sound that remained was the pouring rain.

It didn't sound comforting like the gentle rhythm that made lullabies out of thunderclouds. This rain was different. It felt like grief. Heavy. Relentless. The kind of downpour that blurred the world, smearing memories and moments into water-stained fragments.

Sophia sat curled as tightly as her little limbs would allow. Her spine pressed into the edge of a hard wooden counter, or maybe it was a chair, or the corner of something else entirely. She didn't know. She couldn't tell. Her awareness was folding in on itself, shrinking down to the steady patter of rain on the windows and the reverberate of her own shallow breathing.

Everything else, her grandmother's cries, the man's bloodstained hands, the gasp that had fallen from her lips, had faded into static.

And then there remained complete silence, or just absence. The kind of quiet that leaves behind a ringing, the way you sometimes hear the ocean in a seashell and can't tell if it's real or remembered.

Her hands had gone numb. Her thoughts had unraveled like a spool of yarn dropped on a wet floor. Nothing made sense. Nothing felt real. But one thing pulsed inside her chest with a clarity that cut through everything else: something was gone. Something important.

And it wasn't coming back. Sophia was falling.

Not through space, not through air, but through memory. Through time. Through the kind of grief that leaves a stain on your soul before you're old enough to understand its weight.

And then there was complete darkness. A jolt made her sit up, breathless, and her eyes snapped open. She was twenty-two again.

No longer the wide-eyed girl behind the kitchen counter. No longer dressed in pink pajamas and holding a limp teddy bear in trembling fingers. Now she was a woman, at least by most definitions, but in that moment, lying flat on her back in the darkened loft of her luxury apartment in New York City, she felt just as small as she did all those years ago.

Sophia couldn't move. Her eyes were wide open, but the rest of her refused to obey. Not a single muscle responded.

She wasn't dreaming anymore. She wasn't trapped in a childhood memory. And yet, her body, frozen beneath the duvet, didn't seem to know the difference.

Her brain screamed: move.

Her arms were still, and her legs were paralyzed.

Her lungs worked overtime, pulling in sharp, panicked gasps of air, but everything else remained locked, as though someone had wrapped invisible chains around her limbs and pressed a lead weight into her chest.

The room around her was barely lit , only the soft glow from a streetlamp outside spilled through the wide windows, emitting long, distorted shadows across her ceiling. It was nearly three in the morning. She knew this because the clock beside her bed ticked audibly, cruelly, as if mocking her helplessness.

Sleep paralysis.

It wasn't the first time it had happened. But it never got easier. Each time felt like the first. The terror was always fresh, and the helplessness was always raw.

Her heartbeat thundered in her ears, drowning out even the distant siren wails far below her high-rise. The tightness in her throat was unbearable. She tried to call out , for help, for release, for someone to just tell her she was safe , but her mouth wouldn't open. Not even a whisper escaped.

Just eyes.

Only her eyes could move, darting left and right, looking for something real, something to tether her to the present. But everything looked unfamiliar, distorted, as if the nightmare hadn't entirely let go of her yet.

Her body was awake, but her mind was still somewhere between the dream and the waking world, somewhere she had never truly left.

The dream had returned again. That same one. The night her father died. The night the man came to the door, soaked in rain and guilt. The night her mother was rushed to the hospital and never returned the same.

The night Willow Creek, that quiet, forest-lined countryside town, had stopped being her haven and became a place she could never go back to.

Until now.

She'd been so young then, too young to even grasp what was lost. But the years had a way of collecting reverberates, and now, each birthday, each April rainstorm, each sleepless night, they all brought the memory back like clockwork.

Her body jerked suddenly, a twitch, a gasp, a hiccup of motion that tore through her like a lightning bolt. Her hand shot up to her chest, searching for breath, for safety, for something to hold on to.

The paralysis was gone. The pressure had lifted. But the pain remained.

Her chest rose and fell in uneven bursts, like a swimmer breaking the surface after being pulled under for far too long. She pushed herself upright, the sheets damp with sweat, her nightshirt clinging to her back.

Her skin was cold. Too cold for April.

The plush bear that usually sat on her side table had somehow ended up beside her. She didn't remember grabbing it. Maybe she had it in her sleep. Maybe the version of her in the dream had reached for it , and the adult Sophia had followed without knowing.

She clutched it now, without shame.

It was strange, really. She had survived some of the hardest thing's life could throw at a person: loss, displacement, and emotional abandonment. She had risen from the ashes of her childhood and carved out a life no one believed she could build. A self-made woman in a city that chewed up and spat out the soft-hearted. She was the CEO of a booming finance firm, the name "Sophia Carter" printed on glossy covers and industry blogs alike.

And yet, here she was.

Sitting in the middle of the night, on a king-sized bed in a penthouse suite, holding a teddy bear and struggling not to cry.

That was the thing about trauma. It didn't care about your titles. Or your bank accounts. Or your address.

It waited. It was always lurking patiently until the moment it could crack you open with the same old wound.

The silence was portrayed inside the room like a thick layer. The rain had slowed to a drizzle, but its rhythm still clung to the glass. In a way, it was the only constant. The only thing that had followed her from Willow Creek to New York, from girlhood to womanhood, from innocence to ambition.

She swung her legs over the edge of the bed, wincing as her feet met the cold hardwood floor. She stood slowly, cautiously, as though the room might collapse under her. Her limbs ached, her head throbbed, and her heart hadn't yet returned to its normal rhythm.

She padded barefoot toward the kitchen, flicking on the light and letting the warm amber wash chase the shadows away.

Coffee would help. It always did.

She waited for the machine to brew, and she leaned against the counter, wrapping her arms around herself. Her reflection in the glass of the kitchen cabinets startled her, pale, disheveled, dark circles under her eyes, hair a mess of curls and knots.

She looked like someone she used to be.

Not the polished professional she had perfected into existence, but the broken girl who used to listen to the rain and wonder why the world felt colder when someone stopped loving you.

A soft ding.

The coffee was ready.

She poured it into her favorite mug, a chipped one from a thrift store in Brooklyn, with faded blue sunflowers and a crack near the handle. The mug had no monetary value, but it was one of the few things that had made her feel human over the years.

She took a sip, burning her tongue slightly. But the bitterness grounded her.

And then she saw it.

Something she hadn't noticed before. A cream-colored envelope, sitting neatly on her kitchen counter, right beside the French press. Her fingers hesitated before reaching for it. There was no stamp. No address. Just her name, written in soft blue ink, in handwriting she didn't recognize.

But she felt it in her bones. It was from him. Whoever he was. The one who had been sending the letters. The first had arrived months ago.

Then another, and another, each more intimate, more impossibly accurate than the last. They spoke of things no one else could know. Feelings she never admitted. Memories she thought were buried too deep.

She hadn't told anyone about them. Not even her assistant. Not even the therapist she'd seen three times before, giving up on the idea of healing.

Her fingers trembled slightly as she picked it up. It was heavier than usual.

She didn't open it. Not yet. Instead, she conveyed it to the window, watching as the early morning light began to creep over the skyline. The city, slowly waking up.

The letter sat on the table like it had always belonged there, resting with gentle weight, cream-colored edges curling slightly, touched by the morning air. It hadn't made a sound, hadn't called attention to itself. Yet it had completely consumed Sophia Carter's attention.

Her fingers hovered above it as though touching it would ignite something. She wasn't afraid of words. She had built a life on them , contracts, reports, deals, strategic memos with carefully chosen language that determined the rise and fall of fortunes. But this?

This was different.

She gently unfolded the envelope and pulled the letter free. It was handwritten, as always. No signature. No salutation. Just the same familiar script , slanted slightly, loops confident, pressure steady. Someone who knew how to hold a pen, who took time with their thoughts.

Sophia's breath slowed as she read.

"There's a kind of peace I wish you knew. The kind that lives not in noise or escape, but in stillness, in the breath between things.

The place where I live, time doesn't race. It walks, slowly. The sun doesn't just rise. It stretches, kisses the hills one by one, spills like honey over fields that remember every footstep, every whisper. The mornings here smell like dew and memory, the kind of memory you don't have to explain. It lives in the soil.

There's a tree by the east side of the creek, where the wildflowers gather without needing to be planted. That's where I sit sometimes, when the wind carries music from the chapel on the hill and the leaves shimmer like they're applauding heaven.

I've seen many sunsets from that tree. But never the kind I imagine I'd see if you were there.

I wonder, Sophia, if you remember what it's like to watch the sky bleed slowly into pinks and oranges, not through a plane window or a boardroom's tinted glass, but from the edge of grass-stained jeans and bare feet against cool earth. I wonder if you remember what it's like to be still, completely, in someone's company, not because silence is awkward, but because it's enough.

I wish you could see the way the river glows just before dusk, like it's keeping a secret it's waiting to share. I wish you could see the shadows of birds dancing on the water. I wish you could close your eyes here, with me, and not dream of things to chase, only things to hold.

I wish… I wish you would go back. Not just to nature, but to yourself.

You, who ran with your shoelaces untied and your heart wide open. You, who once believed in stardust and not just spreadsheets. You, who left something behind, when you left to think about your heart. Something important.

Maybe one day you'll remember.

And maybe on that day, you'll sit beside me, and we'll watch the most beautiful sunset in the most beautiful village in the world. Together. Quiet. Full.

Until then, I'll keep watching for you.

Always."

Sophia didn't realize she had stopped breathing until the words ended. Her thumb rested lightly along the edge of the paper, tracing the final line again and again as if the motion might reveal a clue.

She blinked slowly.

Once.

Twice.

And then, without even she knowing about it, a small smile tugged at the corner of her lips, soft, unbidden, like something fragile trying to find its way out of her.

She didn't know what part had made her smile.

Was it the river glowing like it held a secret?

Was it the tree where wildflowers gathered?

Was it the thought of someone, this faceless, nameless someone, sitting in silence with her, not to be impressed or pleased, but simply to be?

She wasn't sure, but the feeling was there.

Brief and confusing.

Because as quickly as it came, she pushed it away.

Sophia closed the letter, folded it with slow precision, and placed it back into its envelope. Her face shifted; shoulders straightened. The softness that had bloomed only seconds ago vanished like a mist burned off by daylight.

She shook her head, scoffing under her breath. "What crap," she muttered.

She stood, poured the rest of her now-lukewarm coffee down the sink, and slid the letter into a drawer, the one with the others.

Letters like this had been arriving for nearly a year now.

At first, she thought it was a prank. Someone's idea of artistic therapy or anonymous romance. But the way the words clung to memories she didn't speak of, the details no public interview had ever contained, it unsettled her.

Still, she'd never thrown one away. Not even once.

Every envelope had been kept, filed, and hidden, and even reread on nights she wouldn't admit to missing something unnamed.

She left the kitchen and returned to her room, where the city beyond her windows had begun to stir. The streets of Manhattan pulsed with life , honking horns, barking dogs, urgent footsteps on rain-slicked sidewalks.

The day had arrived with its usual urgency. Emails waited. Conference calls were scheduled. Deadlines loomed.

But Sophia moved more slowly. The letter had shifted something. Not deeply. Not drastically.

But enough. Enough to make her pause at the closet instead of rushing. Enough to make her look at her reflection a little longer. Enough to make her pick out the lavender blouse instead of the navy one , the one that reminded her of wildflowers for reasons she couldn't explain.

As she dressed, she wondered, but it was not for the first time, who he was. This stranger who wrote to her like he had known her all her life. This voice, who claimed to watch sunsets and remember her barefoot laughter.

She had no time for riddles. She had no space in her life for dreams. And yet… he knew something. Something about her. Something even she had almost forgotten.

She pulled on her coat, grabbed her handbag, and stood by the front door for a moment longer than necessary. Her hand rested on the knob, but her mind was back in Willow Creek, to the creek itself, to the sunsets she hadn't seen in years, to the trees that remembered her better than any person had.

With one last glance toward the drawer, she whispered to herself, "Beautiful village, huh?"

And then she walked out, leaving the letter behind, but carrying the sunset in her mind.

CHAPTER 2: THE BOSS LADY

Sophia Carter stepped out of the elevator with the kind of effortless grace that made heads turn, not from noise or drama, but from something quieter. Something heavier.

Presence.

It wasn't the heels that clicked authoritatively on the marble floor of the 42nd level, nor the tailored graphite gray suit she wore like armor. It wasn't even the sleek black handbag balanced perfectly on her forearm, or the pale rose blouse beneath the blazer that softened the sharp silhouette. No. It was her.

The energy that walked in before her. The silence that followed behind her.

She didn't need to say much. She rarely did. Words, after all, were for people still trying to prove something. Sophia Carter had nothing left to prove.

She was the boss.

She didn't get this all by inheritance or by chance, but by calculated moves, endless nights, and sacrifice carved into her bones. The nameplate on the glass wall behind her office door didn't say CEO just for appearances. She built this company from dust and dared anyone to question her right to rule it.

As she moved past the workstations, every employee stood, not out of obligation, but something more. Respect. A touch of fear. And, for some, a bit of admiration that had nothing to do with her title.

Sophia's beauty was the kind that didn't shout, it murmured, subtle and haunting. Her hazel-blue eyes held a quiet storm that loitered in memory long after the moment had passed. Her skin was porcelain-toned, kissed only by the occasional sunlight that reached her through her office window. She had full, expressive lips that often curved into a small, polite smile, the one that offered nothing and yet disarmed everyone. Her medium height, five-foot-four, didn't make her tower physically, but when she entered a room, space seemed to bend around her anyway.

"Morning, Ms. Carter," her assistant greeted, stepping beside her briskly with an iPad in hand. His name was Nathan Blake, early thirties, crisp brown suit, perpetually overworked but always polished. The only one who had lasted more than six months at her side.

"Your day's packed, as usual," he continued, glancing at the screen. "You've got a final review at 9:30 with the legal team before the merger meeting at eleven. Then a lunch with Mr. Henson from Clearwell Equity at, "

"Cancel the lunch," she said, her voice calm, low, but firm.

Nathan blinked. "Should I, ?"

"Send him something sweet. Apologize on my behalf. Personal reasons," she added as she reached her office door.

"Understood." Nathan didn't press. He never did.

As she stepped inside her office, the door muttering shut behind her, the sound of the city dropped away. Her oasis was an amalgamation of glass, gray stone, and minimal elegance. The skyline stretched out before her, towers, bridges, streaks of life moving below. She turned toward it for a moment, letting the light frame her from behind.

From this view, she looked invincible. But invincibility came at a price.

She slipped off her coat and hung it on the walnut rack, brushing invisible lint from her sleeve. Her posture never broke. Not even when no one was watching.

On her desk, a silver picture frame faced inward, toward her. It held a faded photo of a young girl with wild curls and muddy shoes, sitting on a wooden fence in front of a field in Willow Creek. Her eyes hadn't changed, but her smile back then had reached further. Deeper.

She quickly placed the frame face-down. There was no time for nostalgia in her life; she used to put that down every day, but never removed it from her table. Today, especially when a multi-million-dollar deal waited.

If you ask her, who is your inspiration? She would tell you, her younger self!

An hour later, the boardroom hissed with executives from both companies. Men in sleek suits with expensive pens and nervous eyes. The contract was placed ready in the center of the table like an altar, awaiting sacrifice.

Sophia sat at the head, legs crossed, one hand resting near her coffee, the other flipping through a page.

Nathan stood at her side, tapping on his tablet, but not interrupting. He knew better than to fill silence that wasn't meant to be broken.

"We can move forward on the shared revenue terms," one of the visiting lawyers said, voice trembling slightly under her gaze. "Your team's edits were acceptable, and we uh, we'd be honored to finalize today."

Sophia didn't look up immediately. When she did, she offered the faintest smile.

"The honor," she said, voice silk and steel, "will be mine if you actually deliver on what you promised."

The man nodded too quickly. Another executive chuckled awkwardly. A junior analyst dropped his pen.

Nathan watched her like he always did , half in awe, half in curiosity. She never shouted. Never raised a finger. Yet somehow, she commanded more than any yelling CEO he'd ever met.

The meeting moved forward like a chess match she'd already won last week. Papers were signed. Hands were shaken. People left relieved , and a little breathless.

Back in her office, Nathan followed her in.

"That was clean," he commented, typing a message into his tablet. "I think we just walked out with their best offer."

Sophia sat down behind her desk and sighed, finally.

"Good," she murmured.

He paused. "Still want me to cancel lunch?"

Sophia looked up. "Do I look like I want small talk about market trends over overpriced steak?"

Nathan smirked. "Not in this lifetime."

A pause.

Then she added softly, "Thank you, Nathan."

He blinked, slightly taken aback. "For what?"

"For… understanding."

He gave a small nod and excused himself, leaving her alone once more. She leaned back in her chair, gaze drifting again toward the skyline.

To anyone watching, she had it all , success, admiration, grace, power. But behind the soft smiles and endless achievements was a woman unraveling slowly, quietly.

She spoke less so people would ask fewer questions. She smiled more so no one would see the cracks.

And somewhere between the coffee and contracts, she'd stopped recognizing the girl in the photo frame.

But letters kept arriving.

And some part of her still read them, not because she believed in love stories, or fate, or returns. But because she was beginning to wonder… what if she'd never left Willow Creek completely? What if she had just buried it? And what if someone out there still remembered?

The city melted behind tinted windows as Sophia Carter reclined into the leather of the car's back seat. Evening had unfurled itself across New York like a silk shawl, dotted with golden lights and swaying exhaust fumes. The driver, silent and focused, maneuvered through the usual rush-hour lull while soft jazz played low from the stereo, not loud enough to command attention, but enough to distract her from the storm in her thoughts.

Her phone vibrated. She glanced down at the screen and her eyebrows arched with annoyance, muttering, "Not again", because it was Lucas Wilson.

A deep sigh escaped her lips, not dramatic, but deliberate. She tilted her head slightly, weighing the pros and cons of answering, but she knew she would.

Lucas wasn't like the others. That was both a comfort and a complication. She swiped to answer and placed the phone to her ear.

"Yes, Lucas," she said, voice flat yet warm enough to avoid sounding cold.

"Well, well," came his smooth, slightly amused voice on the other end, "the Queen of the Financial Dominion honors my call. Should I thank the stars or your assistant?"

Sophia allowed herself the hint of a smile. "I don't use the stars. I use calendars."

"Ouch," he laughed. "Remind me to never try poetic metaphors with you."

"Noted," she replied. "Are we talking metaphors today, or do you have numbers that actually matter?"

Lucas chuckled, that familiar confidence seeping into every word. "Straight to business. You never disappoint, Carter."

"You rarely have time to waste," she countered, resting her head back against the leather. "That's why I pick up when it's you."

"Careful," he teased, "flattery might go to my head."

"That wasn't flattery."

"Ouch again. And here I thought I was your favorite stalker."

She didn't laugh, but her lips twitched.

Lucas Wilson was in his early thirties, a CEO of his father's successful tech manufacturing empire, though unlike most "legacy heirs," he didn't flaunt it like a badge of entitlement. He worked. He invested. He showed up on time. He rarely bragged, and when he did, it was self-deprecating and laced with enough irony that she could tolerate it.

Still, she didn't trust him. Not completely. He was a man, after all. And most men, especially those with power, didn't knock on her doors for meetings or calls because they wanted to talk investments. They wanted proximity. And proximity to Sophia Carter had become silent social currency.

But Lucas? He played his part too well. Not too timid, not overly gallant. He was confident. Clean. Dangerous, in a different way.

"I wanted to talk," he continued after a beat, "about the Greenpoint proposal you turned down last quarter."

She raised an eyebrow, surprised. "That was months ago."

"Exactly," he said. "And they've come back , new numbers, better equity ratios. I think they've finally done their homework."

"You're consulting for them?"

"Let's just say I'm watching closely."

Sophia's eyes narrowed slightly, watching the blur of city lights slip past her window. "And what do you want from me, Lucas?"

"Oh, Sophia," he said in a mock-wounded voice, "that's not how friends talk."

"We're not friends."

A pause.

"Right. Sorry. That's not how people with mutual professional respect and occasional sarcasm-laced banter talk."

She huffed quietly, not quite a laugh.

"Anyway," he continued, the charm dimming just slightly into something more serious, "I think this could be a smart move for you. You've got the bandwidth. They've got the tech. And if your portfolio picks up just two more solid AI startups, I'm afraid you'll have to build a second penthouse to stack your success."

Sophia's fingers drummed lightly on her armrest. "You want me to look into them again?"

"I'd like your eyes on it. You don't have to take the deal. But I think it's worth a second glance."

"I don't do second glances."

Lucas went quiet for a moment. "You don't do a lot of things other people do. That's why you're up there while the rest of us crawl."

She didn't respond.

The city was beginning to change , less glass and gloss now, more winding streets and glowing windows. Her home wasn't far.

He continued, his voice softer now. "You ever get tired, Sophia?"

"Of what?"

"Of always winning."

That surprised her. She sat straighter. "Why would I get tired of doing what I worked for?"

He hesitated. "Because you work like you're still proving something. But you already built the empire."

There was something in his tone , something that hinted he saw more than he let on.

She didn't like that.

Sophia exhaled through her nose. "You're drifting off-topic."

"Guilty."

Another pause. Then, lighter: "If you say no, I'll just call again tomorrow. Maybe the day after. I'll bring numbers. Maybe flowers. Or a very expensive bottle of whatever you're allergic to."

"I'm not allergic to anything."

"Even better," he grinned. "Then I'll bring a dozen reasons to like me."

"You already bring too many reasons to be blocked," she said calmly.

Lucas laughed again, delighted. "And yet, you haven't."

Silence stretched between them for a few seconds. Not awkward, just full of unsaid words.

Sophia finally said, "Because you never give me a reason solid enough to."

And that was the truth.

Lucas Wilson, in all his occasional sass and subtle flirtation, never crossed the line. Never asked about her personal life. Never mentioned rumors or appearances or made suggestions he couldn't defend. She could smell ambition from miles away, and flattery, and seduction wrapped in civility. But he had played this dance with discipline.

He spoke business. But under the lines, his eyes sparkled with something else. It was that something else she kept locked out. Every time.

"Well," he said, his voice dropping to a more serious register, "if you ever want to talk outside of business hours… You know where to find me."

"I don't talk outside of business."

"See? That's where you're missing out."

"On?"

"Me."

She didn't answer.

He didn't expect her to.

"I'll send you the revised Greenpoint file," he said at last. "Take your time. Or don't. I'll still be around."

"Goodnight."

"Goodnight, Sophia."

She hung up.

The car rolled quietly into the private lane that led to her building. Her driver stepped out to open the door, and as she climbed out, the wind teased her hair just slightly.

The night stretched out before her. Her castle stood fierce in front of her.

The door opened with a soft magnetic click, and Sophia stepped into the place that technically belonged to her, but had never truly felt like home.

The scent of jasmine and eucalyptus poised slightly in the air, the result of a diffuser she didn't remember buying but let exist anyway. Clean lines, marble floors, and floor-to-ceiling glass greeted her, giving the illusion of space and serenity. Her penthouse, perched on the above floor overlooking Manhattan, was as elegant and meticulous as she was. Everything had its place. Everything had a purpose. No clutter, no chaos.

Yet despite the soft textures and ambient lighting, despite the elegant minimalist furniture and the tasteful placement of designer art pieces, the space felt... incomplete.

Yes, it had everything a house needed, a curated library wall in the study, velvet drapes imported from Florence, a kitchen that gleamed like a magazine spread, and a walk-in closet that many would call a dream. But to Sophia, it lacked one thing.

People.

And because of that, nothing else mattered.

She had never been the type to show off wealth. Her furniture, though expensive, was unbranded. Her crystal vases, though from Paris, bore no tags. She had once told a journalist who featured her in a lifestyle magazine, "The most expensive thing in my house is silence."

It wasn't cynicism. It was true.

Because she knew what it meant to want presence more than presents. And no matter how sophisticated her surroundings, they had never replaced the warmth she longed for when she came home.

Her heels tapped softly against the marble, reverberating in the quiet entryway as her maid approached from the hallway, a middle-aged, soft-spoken woman named Marina, who had been with Sophia for almost six years.

Marina leaned in gently, whispering, "Ma'am... someone's waiting for you in the lounge."

Sophia arched an eyebrow. "Someone?"

Marina hesitated for a moment before adding, "The woman... from a few months ago. The one you helped on the street. She's... she's here."

Sophia nodded slowly, exhaling through her nose. "Thank you, Marina."

Marina followed her as always, a respectful step behind. When they reached the lounge, the soft lighting revealed the shape of a woman rising slowly from the edge of the velvet couch.

Sophia recognized her instantly.

The older woman looked healthier now , fuller cheeks, eyes not as sunken, hair tied back neatly. She wore a modest pale blue shalwar kameez, clean but worn. Her hands were still nervous, fingers twisting the hem of her dupatta. But the bruises that once shadowed her face and arms had faded into memory.

As soon as Sophia stepped into view, the woman bowed her head deeply.

"Hello, madam," she said softly.

Sophia stepped forward. "Hello."

"I hope… I hope you remember me," the woman added nervously.

"I do," Sophia replied, her voice warm but composed. "Please, sit."

The woman hesitated, her feet twitching as if unsure whether she deserved to take up space in such a polished world. Sophia sat first, and only then did the woman lower herself carefully onto the couch once more.

Marina remained nearby, hands folded, posture straight.

"I came to thank you," the woman began, her eyes moist but proud. "I completed my treatment. The medicines you arranged helped more than I can say. And my daughters… they sleep without crying now."

Sophia's expression remained neutral, though her chest tightened.

"I couldn't leave without telling you that I am ready now," the woman continued. "To work. Any work. Anything you allow. I want to earn. With respect."

There was no begging in her tone, only dignity.

Sophia leaned back, studying her. This woman, once broken on a sidewalk, humiliated by the very people she'd served, had returned not for sympathy, but for purpose.

Before Sophia could reply, Marina stepped slightly closer and whispered discreetly near her ear, "Ma'am, she was… accused. Remember? The robbery. Her last employer."

Sophia turned her head just slightly, locking eyes with Marina. And then she said, clearly, calmly, and with an edge that sliced through the room like cold steel:

"Then she understands more than most what it means to be falsely judged."

Marina froze. Sophia turned back to the woman. "What's your name?"

"Samina," she answered, barely above a whisper.

Sophia nodded. "You'll work here. On trial at first, for formality, not suspicion. You'll receive fair pay, proper hours, and no one here will treat you as less than anyone else. Understood?"

Tears filled Samina's eyes, but she blinked them back quickly, nodding, pressing a trembling hand to her heart.

"I… I will never let you down, madam. I swear it."

Sophia shook her head. "Don't swear anything. Just take care of your girls. Do your work. Rest when you're tired. Heal fully."

Marina remained silent, ashamed.

Samina stood up, hands folded before her, and bowed her head again. "Thank you," she whispered, her voice cracking.

Sophia stood too. "We all deserve someone who believes us."

As Samina was gently led by Marina to show her the quarters, Sophia turned toward the wide glass window and watched the city glitter in the distance. Beneath her penthouse sky, she stood with a woman who had nothing left to offer, and she hired her not out of charity, but from memory.

Because once, a long time ago, someone had doubted her too. And if healing meant anything at all… it was that no one should have to walk back into the world alone.

Sophia stood at the tall window, her arms folded across her chest, chin slightly lifted, eyes lost in the expanse of the night beyond. The skyline sparkled in the distance, golden crowns of ambition and endless movement. Yet, her gaze wasn't fixed on the lights. It was in the void between them.

She always stared into that hollow space. The one no skyscraper dared to fill. And then, it started.

The rain.

The first drops struck the glass with the gentleness of memory, which was unsuspecting. But it was enough.

Sophia's heart sank with the sound, her body stiffening the way it always did when that familiar rhythm began. It wasn't fear in the traditional sense. It was recognition. As if her soul responded to the rain with an involuntary pulse of grief, a kind of deep knowing.

She closed her eyes for a second. Just a second. And when she opened them, her breath caught in her throat.

Outside, at the very edge of the roundabout below her building, a dark car had pulled up. The headlights pierced through the mist. The driver's door opened, and an older man stepped out. His frame tall, strong once perhaps, but now bent by something invisible. He moved to the back, opening the door with a slow, careful hand.

A little girl stepped out next. Seven. Maybe eight.

Wearing a pink cotton frock, her hair tied in loose pigtails, one sock pulled higher than the other. She clutched a teddy bear in one hand , worn out, with a patched belly and a missing eye.

Sophia's knees weakened.

The girl's face, pale and lost. Her lips trembling, her eyes wide with a kind of sorrow no child should understand. Her tiny body walked stiffly between the older man and a gray-haired woman, her grandmother, arms stretched protectively behind the girl's back, guiding her gently toward the building entrance.

The little girl looked up. Straight at Sophia. Right through the glass. Through the city. Through time.

And just like that, Sophia's breath disappeared. The bear. The posture. The pale skin. It was her.

Not a stranger. Her.

Sophia stumbled back from the window, a hand to her mouth. Her body trembled not out of fear, but recognition. She closed her eyes again, willing the image to vanish.

When she looked back… Nothing.

No car.

No figures.

No girl.

Just a quiet roundabout, the rain now heavier, washing the scene away like it had never existed.

She leaned her forehead against the glass, her skin cold where it touched. Her heart thudded in her chest.

A hallucination? That's what logic would say.

She was tired. Her sleep was fragmented. Her mind, exhausted by memories she never let fully rise. But hallucination or not, it had been too real.

And worse, it had brought back that day. The one she never spoke of. Not even to her therapist. She was seven years old the day her world shattered.

Hours after that blood-soaked man collapsed in their living room, after the sobs, after the screams, after the prayers... Sophia had found herself seated in the back of her grandfather's car. Her grandfather sat beside her, his face blank, his hands clasped in front of him like he was holding something invisible but heavy. Her grandmother sat on the other side, murmuring verses under her breath.

The car's windshield wipers swayed like pendulums, left, right, left, as though counting down time in a language only storms understood.

Sophia didn't understand where they were going. She only knew it was serious. That no one had changed their clothes. Her grandmother's glasses were still smudged with tears.

The teddy bear in her lap now felt heavy, like it conveyed more than just stuffing.

They arrived at the hospital's emergency wing just past midnight. The lights inside the building were fluorescent, almost too bright for her eyes, but no one seemed to blink. People moved around in a blur of white coats and rubber soles. Machines beeped in the distance. Somewhere, a baby cried.

They didn't let her go inside the ward.

Her grandmother told her to sit on the bench outside. "Just for a minute, darling. Just stay here."

So she did. Feet swinging off the edge. Bear in her arms. Mind a thousand miles away. She remembered the strange smell, that sharp, metallic scent hospitals always held. It made her stomach twist. It didn't smell like healing. It smelled like loss.

Then her grandfather returned. Alone.

She looked up at him. His eyes were red, rimmed like he'd battled wind. His jaw clenched. He kneeled in front of her, and for the first time in her life, he touched her face with shaking hands.

"Your father..." he began, and his voice cracked like glass underweight.

Sophia blinked at him. He didn't say more. He didn't need to.

Her grandmother was in the room behind the glass, curled up in a hospital bed with tubes and wires. Her face was swollen. Her body is still.

Her father was in another room. Not moving. Not breathing. Gone.

That was the night the teddy bear became more than a toy. It became her anchor. Her shield. Her witness.

The hospital's pale blue walls never left her memory. Neither did the nurse who offered her a juice box with trembling hands.

It was the night she forgot how to cry. Not because she didn't feel pain. But because the pain had gone too deep for tears.

Back in the present, Sophia slid slowly to the floor, still sitting by the glass wall, knees drawn to her chest. The rain outside didn't let up. It drummed against the window like a song she hated but knew by heart.

She whispered into the dark, "Why now?"

She hadn't hallucinated like that before.

Was it the letter? Was it the woman she'd helped? Was it… the loneliness?

She couldn't say.

All she knew was the little girl she once was had returned, or perhaps, she never left.

Sophia leaned her head against the glass again. Her reflection stared back at her, 22 years old, successful, powerful, beautiful in the kind of way that made men forget how to speak.

But she didn't see the woman. She saw the girl. The one no one ever asked about. The one who had stopped asking for comfort.

And for the first time in years, Sophia Carter whispered a name she hadn't dared say aloud in a long time.

"Dad…"

Her voice cracked. Just once. And then silence took over again. But not the cold silence of loneliness. This silence was different. This silence… held her.

CHAPTER 3: THE BLOOM BENEATH THE ICE

The rain still hadn't stopped. It hadn't thundered either, just the soft, continuous murmur of water against the glass, like a lullaby she never asked for that stirred old things, and made you listen whether you wanted to or not.

Sophia sat in bed with her legs crossed, a thick cotton robe wrapped around her, her hair loosely tied. A small reading lamp cast a golden pool of light across the pages of the book she'd been pretending to read for the last forty minutes. Her mind, however, had wandered somewhere far beyond New York.

A soft knock reverberated from the door.

"Come in," she said, not lifting her gaze.

Marina entered with her usual grace, a woman of few words and even fewer missteps. She conveyed a silver tray with a steaming cup of black coffee, just the way Sophia liked it before bed. Alongside it rested something cream-colored, folded neatly.

"Your coffee, ma'am," Marina said softly, placing the tray on the bedside table. Then, with a pause, she added, "The guard said this was found in the letterbox just now."

Sophia finally looked up, eyes narrowing at the envelope. The now familiar burden of curiosity pressed into her chest.

Another letter. No address. No sender. Just her name. She reached for it slowly, her fingertips brushing the rough edge before she carefully slit it open.

Marina stopped by the door for a moment longer than usual, but Sophia said nothing. A silent nod dismissed her, and she left.

The moment the door clicked shut, Sophia unfolded the letter.

"You don't know how often your name lives between the thoughts I carry.

I watch the way the world moves around you, how it seems to slow down when you walk into a room, how the air changes when you speak, how even silence seems to listen to you. There is something extraordinary about you, Sophia, something that not even success, beauty, or brilliance could define completely.

It's in the way you keep going when you don't want to. It's in the way your eyes soften before your voice does.

And it's in the way your soul remembers gentleness, even when life forgot to give it to you. I've never seen anyone wear strength so quietly. You think no one notices, how hard you work, how much you've given up, how carefully you love from a distance. But I do. I notice.

I see the burden you carry. I see the grace you wear it with. I see the child in you who once trusted the world, and the woman in you who still hopes it can be trusted again.

There's something about you that makes even a stranger want to protect your peace, to give back to you the softness you were once robbed of.

And if I could, Sophia, I would tell you this:

I want to instill in you every tender truth I've ever known, not just speak it, but live it beside you.

Because you deserve to hear that not everything will leave. You deserve to feel safe in more than just spaces. You deserve to be seen in ways that don't unravel you.

You once said that homes are not made of bricks and beams but of time and touch. I wonder if you've forgotten the place where you first felt both, the place your laughter lived freely, before it became something you measured.

A person should never forget the property where they lived their happiest days. You haven't forgotten it, have you?

The palace.

The one in Willow Creek.

Not the building.

But the feeling."

Sophia's hands went still. Her fingers clutched the edges of the paper so tightly that they trembled. The letter blurred. Not because of the ink. But because of the flood in her eyes.

She swallowed hard and reread one sentence again, her gaze freezing on the line that had struck her like a thunderclap.

"I want to instill in you every tender truth I've ever known."

The words weren't new. Not completely. They had been said before, in a dimly lit room in Willow Creek, on a quiet evening when her grandmother brushed her hair in gentle, patient strokes.

Sophia had been eight. She had sat cross-legged on the floor in front of her grandmother's rocking chair, her wild curls tangled from a day of running through gardens and fields.

Her grandmother, with her slow, delicate hands and eyes full of stars, had hummed softly as she worked through the knots.

"Do you know," she had said, "I want to instill in you every good thing I've ever learned. Every gentle truth I know. So that even when I'm not around, they'll live inside you."

Sophia had giggled then, squirming a little. "Even the secrets?"

"Especially the secrets," her grandmother whispered, kissing the top of her head.

And now, fifteen years later, someone else had written those words. Not in the same voice. Not in the same context. But with the same soul.

A stranger?

Or someone who knew? Her chest tightened. Her mind spun.

She stood up suddenly and walked barefoot toward the window once more, drawn to it as if the answers might live in the rain beyond it. Her reflection shimmered in the glass, eyes wide, a shadow of the girl who once ran barefoot through the hallways of an old stone mansion.

The palace.

She had almost forgotten.

Or had she just buried it?

The grand estate on the edge of Willow Creek, her grandfather's legacy, a place filled with wide open halls, glass chandeliers, and staircases that once reverberated with her laughter. Summers spent climbing trees in the backyard. Winters curled up near the fireplace, listening to old radio stories. A garden that smelled of roses and bread. A room with blue curtains and a window seat she used to read from for hours.

They had called it The Ridge. That was her first real home. The one she had been taken since her childhood. When decisions were made for her. When she was told children don't belong in crumbling estates with broken hearts and fading memories.

And she had left it. Not willingly. But inevitably.

Now, standing in her skyscraper suite in New York City, one of the most enviable addresses in the world, she felt a pang of longing so sharp it made her knees weak.

What if…?

What if she went back?

What would she even find?

She didn't dare answer it. Not yet. But the letter in her hand… it felt like a map. Not to a place. But to a time. A version of herself that still lived somewhere, waiting to be remembered.

She didn't fold the letter.

Didn't tuck it back into the envelope like she usually did. It lay beside her pillow, open and untouched, a tranquil witness to the thoughts flooding her like the rain outside. The words had wrapped around her so tightly that she didn't have the strength to break away from them.

The room was quiet. But her mind wasn't.

She sat upright in bed, her knees pulled up to her chest, arms wrapped around them. Her gaze was fixed not on the letter anymore, but beyond it , on something invisible, something only she could see.

"I've been here before," she whispered to herself.

And she had. Not just in emotion, but in reality. Her thoughts drifted back, uninvited but unstoppable, to a time not too long ago, yet far enough to belong to a younger, more fragile version of herself.

Back when she was just sixteen.

She had been young for an intern, too young, in fact, for most companies to even consider. But Sophia

Carter hadn't been "most teenagers." With a mind that absorbed information like air and an instinct for precision and strategy that startled even seasoned professionals, she'd talked her way into a financial firm in midtown Manhattan.

It had been a sweltering summer when she started, the kind of heat that clung to your skin, but that particular evening, the skies had shifted. Heavy clouds had rolled in, and the light drizzle that began during her lunch break had transformed into a full-fledged storm by the time her shift ended.

She was supposed to be home before dark. She always was.

But work had run late. Her manager had asked her to stay back to rework a report, impressed by her meticulousness. Sophia, eager to prove herself, hadn't hesitated. She left the building just before eight, alone, umbrella-less, and too stubborn to call anyone.

The streets were glossy with rain, reflections shimmering like broken mirrors. Her heels tapped against the pavement with rhythmic precision, and her blazer clung to her shoulders as the downpour intensified.

She turned the corner onto 52nd Street.

That's when she saw him.

Her steps faltered.

Just ahead, standing beneath a gleaming streetlamp, was a tall man in a navy coat and a flat cap, his silver-white hair unmistakable beneath it. His stance was familiar. His hands tucked behind his back; his chin slightly lifted. His shoes still polished like he used to keep them every Sunday morning.

Her grandfather. Sophia's breath hitched. He was standing in the exact posture he used to take while waiting for the postman in Willow Creek, next to the gates of their estate.

She blinked rapidly, the rain distorting her vision, but he didn't vanish. His face was clear. Pale. Eyes shadowed. He looked directly at her.

Sophia stepped forward.

Her heart wasn't pounding in her chest anymore, instead, it was stopping. Slowing. As if her body didn't know whether to flee or fall.

"Grandpa...?" she whispered.

But no voice came out.

She was halfway across the street when she realized she had stopped breathing.

He didn't move. Just stared, neither coldly nor warmly. Just kept his eyes on her.

And that's when it happened. A sound behind her.

The faintest scuffle of feet. The shuffle of shadows. She turned too late.

Three boys, no older than twenty, emerged from the alley. Wet hoodies, sneakers soaked, grins stretched thin across their faces. One of them conveyed a bottle. Another had his hands in his jacket, as if hiding something.

Sophia didn't scream. She didn't run.

Because her mind was still with her grandfather, the impossible image of him pulling her under a spell so deep she hadn't noticed the danger approaching.

One of the boys whistled.

"Hey, little boss lady," he mocked, his voice low and oily. "Out late, huh?"

She took a step back. They closed in. Panic surged too late. One grabbed her arm. Another yanked her shoulder bag.

She struggled, twisted, pushed, but they laughed.

"Let's calm her down," one of them muttered.

Then came the shove. The world spun.

Her knees slammed against the pavement, a sharp jolt of pain tearing through her leg. Rain soaked her through. The teddy bear keychain from her bag skidded across the wet sidewalk. Her breath came in shallow gasps. Her vision blurred not from rain, but from terror.

She thought she might faint.

She thought …

Then came the sound. A growl. Metal and thunder.

A motorbike roared through the narrow street like something summoned.

All three boys looked up. The rider sat on the thick bike, stopped inches away. He wore a Black helmet, leather jacket, and gloves. His sudden presence in the scene didn't ask for permission, just commanded it. He didn't speak. Didn't need to.

He moved fast. Like he'd done this before.

One of the boys lunged, swinging something, a bottle? A chain?

But the rider ducked. Grabbed the arm mid-air. Twisted. There was a crack. A scream. A kick that sent the second flying into the trash bins.

Sophia couldn't see clearly anymore.

All she knew was that the mess had reversed itself.

The boys who were pretending brave a second ago were now crawling away, limping, cursing, scattering into the night like rats.

The rider turned toward her. She looked up. Rain streaming down her face. Breath heaving.

He didn't approach. Didn't offer a hand. He just nodded, slowly, as if telling her: It's done. You're safe.

Then he sped off, tires screeching as the bike melted into the rain and smoke of the night.

And Sophia?

She ran. Didn't stop to thank him. Didn't scream. Didn't cry. She just ran as fast as possible with non-rhythmic breathing until the lights of her apartment building welcomed her like a lighthouse to a sinking ship.

She'd collapsed in her room that night, shaking uncontrollably. The hallucination of her grandfather had dissolved somewhere in between the thudding of boots and the roar of that bike. She never told anyone. Not even her therapist, or anyone around. Not even herself, not out loud.

But she never forgot.

And now, all these years later, that memory came back. Sophia blinked back to the present, sitting now with her arms wrapped around her knees.

"I was too young," she whispered to the letter on her pillow. "Too alone."

She didn't know who that rider was. She didn't know why her grandfather had appeared. But something in her heart said it wasn't random. Nothing in her life ever had been.

The next morning in Sophia Carter's penthouse was fresh, sterile, and tranquil like all other mornings, just as she preferred it. Her windows, shaded in soft ivory linen, filtered the sunlight into muted golds that gently kissed the marble floor of the lounge. She emerged from her room already dressed for the day, fitted beige slacks, a soft pastel blouse, heels that reverberated faintly with each step, and her hair twisted into a loose, effortless knot at her nape.

She seemed Immaculate, composed, and flawless as always. She wasn't one to loiter in the mornings. Her routine was sharp and minimal. Shower, dress, coat. A ghost drifting through domesticity. But Marina, ever insistent and persistent in her kindness, had made breakfast a quiet ritual she refused to let Sophia abandon.

This morning was no different. As Sophia descended into the lounge and walked toward the dining area, she saw Marina's hunched figure rushing to set the table, warm toast, fresh-cut fruit, a poached egg, and chamomile tea. Marina's fingers worked with delicate urgency, her bun slightly lopsided, and the apron around her waist flour-stained.

"You don't need to …" Sophia began softly, pausing mid-step.

Marina, still not facing her, interrupted gently, "You'll take a few bites, ma'am. That's all I ask. Just a few."

Sophia sighed, saying nothing, but her feet took her forward. She didn't sit for herself. She sat for Marina. She always did.

Not because she enjoyed breakfast. Not because her stomach ever allowed it. But because someone, even quietly, even cautiously, cared about her. And when that care came without expectation, she didn't have it in her heart to reject it.

She seated herself with all the poise of a monarch attending a meeting of the board, her cold composure unbending even in domestic simplicity. She reached for a slice of toast, broke off a small corner, and nibbled silently, her eyes distant, her mind far from the table. Until they landed on the bouquet. It hadn't been there the night before.

A large arrangement of pale pink roses, baby's breath, and lavender lilies sat elegantly in the center of the table. Dew still clung to the petals. Tucked delicately among the flowers was a folded card.

Sophia froze. Her hand halted mid-air, the piece of toast slipping quietly onto the plate again. She leaned forward, her eyes narrowing slightly. Her fingers, suddenly cold, reached for the card.

It was small. Just two lines, handwritten in smooth, confident script.

"Happy Birthday, Queen."

No name. No signature. Just that. Her breath caught in her chest.

Another letter? Could it be from… him? Could it be from the same secret admirer who had been sending her letters for years?

Was this the first time he had sent something tangible? The thoughts hadn't even finished forming in her mind when Marina, now returning from the kitchen with a napkin, noticed the expression on her employer's face.

"Oh," she said casually, wiping her hands, "that was delivered early this morning, ma'am. From Sir Lucas. He sent it with the same chauffeur who usually brings their files for signature."

Sophia looked up sharply.

The card trembled slightly between her fingers.

"Lucas…?"

"Yes," Marina replied. "Lucas Wilson, I think? From the Silva project , the international equity group. He's the one who always wears the gold cufflinks."

Sophia didn't reply. She didn't breathe.

The words blurred before her eyes. Her heartbeat pulsed in her ears like a war drum.

Lucas Wilson?

Lucas?!

Her mind raced back through every moment she had ever spent with him, boardrooms, formal dinners, shared discussions over global funds and negotiation terms. He was professional. Polite. Handsome, in the way many successful men were. Always mild, always clear, always calm.

But personal?

Never.

Never once had he crossed a line. Never once had he spoken to her about anything except work, and briefly, travel, wine, and politics, when business dinners demanded small talk.

And yet, he had written "Queen"?

The same name used in the anonymous letters? Was it him? Was it Lucas all along? No, her mind screamed. No , he couldn't have written those letters. He didn't know…

He didn't know about Willow Creek.

About her grandfather. About the hospital hallway. About the bear. Her knees stiffened. Her spine locked. A cold ripple coursed through her veins.

If Lucas was the one sending her letters, then how could he have known things no one else did? How could he possibly understand memories she had buried in places she'd never even spoken about?

Was he spying on her? Was it all a calculated plot? Was he just like the rest of them, masked better, quieter, more patient?

Her pulse rang in her ears. She couldn't move. Couldn't speak.

Marina, sensing the shift in the air, placed a small saucer in front of her. A single cupcake sat atop it , no icing, just warm vanilla with a tiny gold candle beside it.

"I didn't know it was your birthday, ma'am," Marina said quietly, hesitantly. "If I had known sooner, I would've made something special. But this… this was all I could do with the time I had. I hope it's okay."

Sophia turned her face toward her slowly. Her eyes, though shaken, softened. For a moment, the storm quieted. She looked at the small cupcake.

At the trembling hands of the woman who'd remembered her in a way no calendar or assistant had.

It was imperfect. Plain but real.

Sophia reached out and touched Marina's hand gently.

"You remembered," she spoke in a low voice, "that was enough."

Marina's eyes watered, but she smiled. "You deserve at least that."

And just for a moment, Sophia wished the bouquet wasn't on the table. Wished the card wasn't real. Wished the letters had come from someone who knew her, not someone who just saw her from across a boardroom.

But inside her, something snapped into awareness.

If it was he … Then she had been fooled. And that… she would not forgive.

She didn't wait for her coat. Or her phone. Or a breath. She stormed out like a woman with lightning pulsing through her veins. Not a single word left her lips as she passed the lounge, the vase of lilies, the cupcake Marina had shyly placed by her untouched breakfast. There was no glance back. No hesitation.

Only fury. Pure, cold, and magnificent.

She wasn't wearing rage, she was rage. Dressed in cream slacks and a high-collared blouse that fluttered behind her like a cape in the wind, Sophia Carter looked like a storm given skin.

Marina called from behind, "Ma'am? Are you?"

"Driver," Sophia said, already heading to the elevator. "Now."

Marina didn't press. The look in Sophia's eyes made even questions scatter for shelter. By the time she reached the driveway, Imran had barely pulled the car to a stop when she slid in, her voice slicing through the air.

"Lucas Wilson's office. Now."

Imran, her driver, blinked and startled. She had never raised her voice before. Never gave sudden orders. Never erupted.

But something in her tone sent shivers down his spine. He didn't ask. He just nodded and drove.

And as he drove, faster than he'd ever dared on Manhattan streets, Sophia sat in the back seat, fists clenched, breath sharp, mind a whirlwind of memories and disbelief.

Lucas Wilson. Him? How dare he?

How dare he hide behind anonymity and write those letters? How dare he slip into her life so gently, so cleverly, pretending to be the only man who never tried to charm her, when he'd been doing it all along?

How could he? Did he think she wouldn't notice? That she wouldn't realize?

Sophia Carter, the woman who burned every weakness in herself and walked proudly over their ashes, played by a man who sent her riddles dipped in affection? Who used words like armor, poetry like poison?

He thought she was soft? He thought he could reach her heart?

She was unreachable. Unshakeable. She had been shattered and rebuilt in the dark, piece by piece, with no one's hand but her own. No love letters. No confessions. No saviors.

Her wrath was silent. Elegant. And today, she was unstoppable.

"Faster," she said again.

Imran looked in the mirror, hesitant, but obeyed.

When they arrived, the towering Wilson International headquarters stood glassy and grand , but it could've been made of sand for all she cared. Because today, she was ready to tear it down with a look.

Sophia stepped out before the car fully stopped. Heels cracking against marble. Air tightening around her. People noticed immediately.

Sophia Carter came unannounced. Untamed. She didn't slow. She didn't breathe. Every step toward the building's heart was a war drum. Assistants stood. Security whispered.

A secretary at the front desk gasped. "Ms. Carter? Do you have a …"

Sophia didn't even look at her, didn't reply because she didn't even need to. She was the appointment. She was the reason people cleared their schedules.

She marched through glass hallways with the force of a woman scorned, not by love, but by betrayal. And that was worse.

The moment she turned the final corner, Lucas's executive secretary stood abruptly from her desk.

"Ms. Carter, I, he's on a call …"

Too late. Sophia flung the door open. And there he was.

Lucas Wilson, charming as ever, phone in hand, mid-sentence. "What? No, I said …"

His eyes landed on her. Everything stopped. His voice died. The phone dropped.

Sophia Carter stood before him like fury carved from marble, like justice wrapped in silk, like fire in high heels. He had seen her in meetings. He had spoken to her for months. But he had never seen her like this.

This close. This furious.

"Miss Sophia…?" he managed, stunned.

"What startled you now?" She asked with fury deposited in her voice.

"I have never seen such a beautiful and passionate woman from such a close view!" He spoke with a grin, trying to lighten the increasing tension in the air, but instantly realized it was not the right time for jokes.

"You sent the bouquet." A statement, not a question.

He blinked. "I, yes. It's your birthday. I thought …"

"And the letters?" she snapped, voice cold as ice.

Lucas's brow furrowed. "What letters?"

Sophia stepped closer. She had never been more terrifying. Or more beautiful. "Don't lie to me."

"I'm not, what letters?"

She stared at him, eyes narrowing like daggers. "The anonymous ones. The ones I've been receiving for almost a year. The ones that know things no one should know."

His expression shifted, from confusion to realization to alarm. And then he shook his head.

"And what made you think I would ever send such childish stuff?"

She didn't move. Didn't blink. She searched his face, every muscle, every twitch, every breath.

"And how can I even imagine that you could be played with just some foolish letters? As far as I know, Sophia Carter can't be played with emotional drama!"

And she just realized that he wasn't lying. He wasn't the writer. He wasn't the man behind the letters. It was a misunderstanding. It didn't take her too long to calculate ever in her life. It was a blessing in the current situation, but a curse in the morning when she calculated too early that it must be from him too, just because the bouquet was from him.

And for a moment, the silence was so deep it rang in her ears. She stepped back.

Lucas watched her, still stunned. "What's going on?"

But she didn't answer. Because suddenly, the truth felt even heavier. It wasn't Lucas. But someone out there knew her.

CHAPTER 4: AN UNINVITED GUEST

Silence wrapped around the room like smoke after a fire.

Lucas Wilson stood frozen for a moment, his hand hovering above the receiver, mouth slightly parted, brows furrowed as if trying to process the storm that had just torn through his office. Sophia Carter, in all her fire and elegance, stood in front of him , but not with the same fury as before.

Her shoulders were still tense. Her breath still sharp. But something was shifting. Her gaze had softened , not entirely, but just enough to reveal confusion beneath the rage.

She stared at him, eyes locked.

And then, in a quieter voice that trembled with something she hadn't yet named, she asked, "How do you know it's my birthday?"

Lucas didn't answer immediately. And for the first time in their entire acquaintance, he didn't have a smirk ready. His confidence paused. Not cracked, just recalibrated.

He blinked, tilted his head slightly, then allowed the corners of his lips to lift into a crooked, unbothered smile.

"You know, Miss Carter," he said, reaching down to adjust his cufflink with infuriating calmness, "I told you once… I keep an eye on things I find important."

Sophia didn't blink. He stood upright again, brushing invisible dust off his already immaculate blazer.

"It was just a matter of a few taps," he added casually, "and a few calls. Your ID records, some old document databases, your internship applications… birthdays are mentioned in a dozen places, Madam."

Then came the part that made her eyes narrow.

He grinned. "Yeah. That's a different case; nobody notices it. Just the people like me."

He shrugged. "I noticed. Yes."

Sophia said nothing. She wanted to believe it was a harmless explanation. She almost did. But the swirl in her stomach told her she wasn't quite ready to trust it. Not yet.

Lucas, still unbothered, gestured toward the chair in front of him. "Have a seat, Miss Carter."

She crossed her arms. "I don't plan on staying."

He raised a brow and, in one fluid motion, sat down behind his desk, folding his hands like a man about to broker peace after war.

"Well," he said with mock solemnity, "if you blow out of my office the same way you stormed in… people might question what happened."

Sophia didn't flinch. Lucas leaned forward a little, lowering his voice with theatrical gravity.

"And I know you don't like… scandals."

She stared at him, unimpressed. He smiled again, more softly now. "Relax. I'm not going to haunt you with any foolish romantic scripts. No roses, no sonnets, no late-night calls with metaphors."

That made her exhale. Not quite a laugh. But not silence either.

She sat. Slowly.

Still stiff, still alert, still composed, but seated nonetheless. Lucas watched her for a moment, then leaned back with the easy comfort of a man who'd survived far more terrifying boardroom confrontations.

Sophia lowered her gaze, her fingers fidgeting for half a second before stilling again.

She was thinking.

She had overreacted.

And worse, she had exposed something. She had told him… about the letters. About a secret that had lived behind locked doors in her mind for over a year.

He didn't ask. He didn't poke.

But she could feel the weight of her own words hanging in the air. She had been reckless. She had shown her hand.

Oh God.

How mad she had been. She wasn't the kind of woman who lost control. She wasn't the kind who accused without knowing. She wasn't the kind who showed her scars to people who hadn't earned the right to see them.

And yet she had done all of that. Because of a bouquet. Because of one line on a card.

"I don't appreciate being played with," she said finally, her voice low, ice swirling beneath her words. "So I'll make this simple. If I ever find out you had anything to do with those letters , with any attempt to pry into my life, if you even thought of it..."

She leaned forward, her eyes burning into his.

"I will set your empire on fire."

Lucas didn't move. He didn't laugh either. He just nodded slowly. And said something that made her still.

"I wouldn't try to steal something from someone I want to earn."

Sophia blinked.

He added, "And I don't deal in fire. I deal in time."

She stared at him. Confused. Caught. Just for a second.

She didn't understand what he meant. Not fully. But she felt something shift inside her. The threat in her throat dissolved before she could speak it. She sat back. She didn't know whether she'd won the argument. Or lost something else entirely.

Lucas, sensing the shift, didn't push. He picked up his phone again, pressed a button, and turned to the glass window beside them.

"Would you like coffee before you leave?" he asked casually. "Or just want to check for more emotional crimes on your way out?"

Sophia exhaled sharply. Not a laugh. But something dangerously close.

"Don't push it," she said.

He grinned. "Wasn't planning to."

And yet, as she stood, and walked to the door, and paused with her hand on the handle, she heard his voice behind her.

Not mocking. Not flirty. Just quiet.

"You know, Sophia… perhaps those letters, whoever is writing them, is not a threat, perhaps, the writer might only want to … express his admiration. Anyways, tell the audience of today's show that it was a minor emergency meeting to lock a sudden deal."

She didn't turn. She didn't answer. But her fingers gripped the door tighter than before.

"Well, Miss Carter never walked into someone's office herself, so it's hard they would believe!" He sighed, and a bittersweet laughter escaped his lips.

And when she left the room, the click of her heels sounded less like a departure… And more like a reverberation.

Her office was silent as she walked and placed her belongings on the table, locking the door for a few minutes. She stood alone beside the enormous glass window that stretched from floor to ceiling, framing the endless sprawl of New York City like a painting that could never be finished. Beyond the skyline, clouds had begun to gather again, darkening the buildings below, as if reverberating the shadows pooling in her mind.

Her coat hung limply behind her chair, the only part of her that had softened today. She hadn't moved in a while. Her hands were folded, arms loosely wrapped across her chest, her gaze far off and fixed on something invisible. Her breath moved slowly, deliberately, not out of peace, but control.

The truth was… she was tired. Not from meetings. Not from confrontation. But from thinking.

Today had taken something out of her. Not just energy. Not just pride. Something deeper. Something she didn't even know had a name.

It was a feeling she hadn't tasted in years. "Fear."

And it didn't come with sirens or screams. It came with silence that curled under her skin and murmured in her ears, What if you're not as in control as you think?

This morning had shaken her not because she had been wrong about Lucas but because being wrong meant one thing for certain: She had no idea who was right.

The person behind the letters was still out there.

Still watching. Still writing. And now, more than ever, she realized… They knew her. Too well. Too precisely. She had long ignored the fact that what if the writer is someone she does not want to let know that much about her past or anything about her? She realized this point just today.

She had never feared people. Not the men who admired her, not the ones who pretended to love her ambition while fearing her power. Not the competitors.

Not the liars. Not even the ones who dared to challenge her in boardrooms.

But the man, or person, behind those letters? They didn't challenge her. They didn't ask anything from her. And maybe that's what scared her most.

Because only people who want nothing… hold the power to take everything.

Sophia exhaled slowly, pressing her forehead against the cool glass for a brief second. She was not afraid of being alone. She was afraid of being known.

And the writer, whoever he was, knew parts of her that even she had tried to forget. He knew about Willow Creek. About her grandmother's lullabies. About the Creekside tree she used to sit under. About her fear of storms. Her scars.

What did he want? Why now?

She pulled away from the glass and walked slowly back to her chair. Her fingers ghosted over the back of it, brushing the edge of her coat, and she sat down, the weight of the room sinking into her shoulders.

Her heart had stopped racing hours ago. But her mind hadn't stopped running.

What if… What if he knew more? What if he wasn't writing out of admiration?

What if he was watching? What if he was trying to use what he knew? To manipulate her? To blackmail her? To own her, not with chains or threats, but with words?

She hated that she didn't know. She hated the not knowing more than anything else.

Control, that was her fortress. That was her signature. That was how she moved through the world untouched. And now someone was in. Without permission. Without invitation.

She rubbed her temple and reached for a folder on the desk, not to read it, but to ground herself in something, anything, routine.

But it didn't work. Her mind kept returning to one thought. *What if it's someone I wouldn't want knowing me?*

Because here's the thing about trauma. It doesn't just leave scars. It teaches you to vet every face. To question every kindness. To build walls so high, even the stars stop sending light.

And she had worked so hard to live above it all. But the letters were a rope. A silent, silken thread pulling her back down.

She stood again, restless now, walking slowly across the room to her bookcase. She didn't even look at the titles. She just traced the spines with her fingertips, trying to feel something that didn't ache.

But the ache was there. And this time, it wasn't from the past. It was from the present. From not knowing who had looked inside her and decided to write back.

She wanted to believe it was romantic. She did. But Sophia Carter didn't have the luxury of romance. She didn't have space for vulnerability that wasn't hers by choice. And now she realized: someone had taken it.

She sat again, slowly. Her knees weak, though no one would ever know. She stared at her reflection in the glass. Her face, serene and beautiful. Her eyes, unreadable.

But inside, she whispered to herself, You're afraid. Not of the world.

Not of failure. But of being seen. Because what if the person behind those letters wasn't just a stranger? What if he was someone close? Someone who had watched. Who had stayed in her orbit for long enough to memorize the map of her?

What if… she had already trusted him? Her stomach twisted. She needed to know. Not because she was curious. But because she had to regain control. She couldn't live in this limbo. She needed to unmask the mystery. She needed the truth. Before it reached deeper. Before it touched parts of her that she couldn't protect anymore.

She needed to know if he was dangerous. Or worse… If he was sincere.

Because Sophia Carter could fight liars. She could silence manipulators. But sincerity? That was her weakness. And she had no armor left for that.

And there, she decided! She decided that she was going back to Willow Creek!

She was going back. Back to Willow Creek, to the place she once called home , not for closure or nostalgia, but for truth. And perhaps… for answers she had long been too afraid to search for.

And once that decision rooted itself in her heart, there was no room left for indecision. No moment wasted on doubt.

She turned around with the speed that made her chair creak. Her coat , still hanging behind it , was yanked off in one motion. She shrugged it on and reached for her bag and laptop, her movements quick, purposeful, urgent.

With each step toward the door, her thoughts grew clearer. Her breaths came deeper.

She pushed the intercom. "Nathan, come in."

Seconds later, her office door opened, and in stepped her trusted assistant, Nathan, impeccably dressed as always in a gray suit, iPad tucked under one arm, and an expression that immediately changed to concern when he saw her face.

He was used to seeing her composed. He wasn't used to seeing her decided, not like this.

"You called, ma'am?"

"Yes. I need you to listen carefully," she said, already stacking documents into her leather tote.

He blinked, stepping closer. "Of course."

"For the next ten days, I'll be off. I need you to cancel the internal compliance review meetings, push the marketing syncs to next week, and hold the quarterly wrap presentation until I return. Also, take all scheduled

Zoom calls with our international clients on my behalf. The investment summit panel? Mark yourself as attending for the firm."

Nathan stared. For a few beats too long.

Then finally, "Ma'am… where are you going?"

"I'm heading home," she said, calm as the sea just before a hurricane.

"Home?" His voice almost cracked. He quickly tapped his screen. "But ma'am, it's just 10:30, and you have your second investor call in fifteen minutes. After that, there's a legal team lunch. You mentioned a strategy meeting for the restructuring committee, and then there's the …"

"I said cancel them," she interrupted, brushing past him toward the door.

Nathan followed her, clearly flustered now. "But ma'am … ten days? That's… that's a long time. Why are you… why are you telling me to cover that long a gap?"

Sophia didn't stop walking. She was halfway down the hall when she replied, "Because I'm taking time off."

There was silence behind her for a moment. Then came his voice again, this time higher, completely stunned.

"Wait… you're taking off?"

She turned slowly, a single brow raised, eyes cool and steady.

Nathan, realizing his tone, cleared his throat and straightened his posture. "I, I mean, of course, yes, you deserve it. It's just… I thought maybe this was an emergency."

Sophia said nothing. Just looked at him. And that stare said everything.

He swallowed, then offered a half-apology through a nervous laugh. "Sorry, I guess I'm just… surprised. You've never taken leave. Not even for a weekend."

"I know," she said.

And then, just as she was about to step into the elevator, she turned her head again, voice calm but commanding.

"One more thing, Nathan."

He looked up from his iPad. "Yes, ma'am?"

"Book a seat for me," she said, pausing just long enough for the impact of the next words, "to Willow Creek."

Nathan's fingers froze over the screen.

He blinked once. Twice.

"I, I'm sorry, did you say… Willow Creek?"

Sophia nodded, lips barely parting as she adjusted the strap of her bag on her shoulder.

"I thought you'd be heading to a beach somewhere," he said with a nervous chuckle. "You know… Thailand, Maldives, private resort in Greece. Maybe a yacht. Not, well, not Willow Creek. I mean, that's a small,"

"I didn't ask for your suggestion," she cut in, not harshly, but with a firm finality that made the entire hallway freeze.

Nathan looked like he'd just been hit with a gust of wind.

He straightened. "Yes, ma'am."

"I want a first-class seat on the earliest Amtrak train to Lancaster," she added, adjusting her coat. "From there, book a cab or local transport. I know there's no direct service to Willow Creek. You can use my travel profile."

Nathan began tapping furiously.

"You'll need to leave from Penn Station," he muttered as he worked. "Train in two hours. Transfer from Lancaster County via a local service, should be less than an hour by road."

"Good," she replied.

Then, almost as an afterthought, she turned back toward him.

"And don't send any emails. Don't announce anything. Tell everyone I'm attending a private conference overseas. That's all they need to know."

Nathan nodded, stunned silent but too professional to question further.

As she stepped into the elevator, the doors slowly sliding shut between them, he caught her last words.

"Oh, and don't try to reach me. If I want to be contacted, I'll contact you."

The doors closed. Back in the silence of the descending elevator, Sophia closed her eyes.

Her heart was racing but it was not fear that caused bradycardia, it was delusional expectations. She had never told anyone at the office about Willow Creek. Not even Nathan, who had been with her through every empire she built, every scandal she dodged, every summit she led.

It wasn't a place she advertised. Because it wasn't a place, it was a story she hadn't dared re-read. But now she was going back. Back to the quiet streets. Back to the house with the green shutters.

Back to the field where her grandfather used to read aloud to her from the newspaper. Back to the creek where she had once buried her teddy bear after the hospital night.

She didn't know what she would find there. But she knew what she was leaving behind.

Doubt. Fear. Questions without faces.

Because if the answers lived anywhere, it was there. In the soil that remembered her. In the wind that once held her name. In the silence that no longer frightened her.

As the car rolled through the city, the towering buildings flashing by like the pages of a book she was about to close for a while, Sophia leaned her head against the window. The coolness of the glass grounded her, and her breath fogged the lower edge as her thoughts drifted, not forward, not sideways, but back.

Back to Willow Creek. Back to The Ridge.

And before she realized it, her lips began to curl into a smile , not the kind she offered in meetings or to the press, not the social curve she gave to photographs or polite dinners. This was slower, deeper, the kind of smile that didn't come from happiness, but from remembrance.

She could see it all in her mind.

The Ridge, her grandfather's house, wasn't enormous by today's standards, but it didn't need to be. It stood with dignity, with quiet grandeur, perched elegantly atop the natural elevation that gave it its name. The way it loomed over the sloping hills made it look regal without being gaudy, a watchtower over the village that watched back with love.

Its walls were smooth stone and timber. The shutters were once a deep forest green, weathered now, no doubt, but back then always freshly painted. The flower beds were modest but well-kept. No fountains, no imported marble, no unnecessary embellishments, and yet it had the kind of timeless elegance that only comes from care, purpose, and pride.

Her grandfather was the same.

Sophia's smile widened, slowly stretching across her face as if it had been asleep for years and was finally waking up.

He was one of the wealthiest men in Willow Creek, yes. But wealth had never made him proud. It had made him responsible. He believed that money was just another language, one that should be spoken to serve, not separate.

And so he did. He built wells when the summers dried the creeks. He repaired roofs for widows who couldn't afford repairs. He paid for textbooks, for medicine, for small businesses trying to breathe. He was not a politician. But they called him the king of the village.

Because every issue, from family feuds to farmland disputes, somehow ended up at his doorstep, and he listened. Always. With a firm hand on his cane and soft eyes behind his glasses, he listened, and then he guided, not with control, but with compassion.

People didn't just trust him. They loved him.

And though he never decorated The Ridge with gold or imported chandeliers, its halls held the laughter of children he fed and the prayers of families he helped. His legacy wasn't etched into plaques or statues , it lived in stories, in small gratitude-filled eyes, in the way people still spoke of him like he was an era, not just a man.

Sophia remembered holding his hand as a girl, walking the garden path that led from the gate to the porch. She remembered how tightly he held her fingers, how she'd count the ridges of his knuckles with her thumb. He smelled like mint and old books. His pockets always conveyed a handkerchief, a pen, and one sugar candy, always for her.

She used to sit on the edge of the stone porch, watching sunsets with him, while he shared stories about the village's history, his own childhood, and sometimes, just made-up fairy tales with dragons and girls who weren't afraid of anything.

And now… She was going back to the Ridge. To him. To a version of herself that she feared was long gone.

She didn't know if the house still stood exactly as it was , if the furniture had faded, if the windows still creaked at night. But it didn't matter. She needed to see it. To stand at the top of that path again. To breathe the same air he breathed. To remember who she had been before the world demanded she become someone else.

Her heart ached, but it was a beautiful ache. And just as her smile widened, it warmed the very edges of her eyes but suddenly she noticed something and her eyes landed to the rearview mirror.

Imran, her driver's eyes had shifted from the road to the mirror… and stayed there a second too long.

Their eyes locked.

She saw that unmistakable expression of curiosity in his eyes, Surprise.

He had caught her smiling. Smiling for no visible reason. And he was clearly startled. Sophia's smile vanished instantly. Her spine straightened. Her eyes cooled.

She turned her head away from the mirror and looked sharply out the window once more, her jaw tightening just slightly.

The moment was gone. Shut back into the same drawer where she kept all emotions, she didn't authorize others to witness. Imran quickly adjusted his gaze, eyes darting back to the road, clearing his throat.

Neither of them said a word.

But the silence said everything. Sophia Carter did not smile without cause. And no one , no one , ever saw her without her armor.

Just for a second, And just like that, the fortress rebuilt itself around her. Because memories were welcome.

But vulnerability? That stayed locked.

CHAPTER 5: HER LOVE LANGUAGE

The reverberate of heels striking marble announced her return long before she stepped into the lounge. The door had barely clicked shut behind her when Marina came rushing in, breathless, the edge of her apron fluttering with each hurried step.

It was just past 11 a.m., and Sophia Carter, the woman who orchestrated billion-dollar negotiations and rarely, if ever, returned home before sundown, was suddenly back, just two hours after leaving with an expression that could set forests on fire.

Marina had been wringing her hands all morning, guilt wrapped tightly around her like her own apron. She had barely spoken to the other staff, her mind racing with questions. Had she offended her? Was it something she said? Was the cupcake a foolish idea?

Sophia's storming departure had left her rattled, her own eyes stinging with unshed tears as she watched the elevator doors close that morning. She had prayed, in inaudible murmurs, for forgiveness, even without knowing the crime.

Now, seeing Sophia Walk back into the house unexpectedly, her coat still hanging loosely on her shoulders and her hair undone slightly from the wind outside, Marina felt a lump rise in her throat.

She stepped forward instantly. "Ma'am, ma'am, please, forgive me, if I said something, or did something, please believe me I didn't mean to offend you, I didn't know the cupcake would upset you, "

Sophia blinked, caught mid-step in the hallway, and for a moment, she looked completely puzzled. Then, understanding flooded her face like sunrise melting away fog. Her expression softened completely, and something almost tender passed through her eyes.

She stepped forward and gently placed a hand on Marina's shoulder, stopping her mid-sentence.

"Marina," she said softly, her voice gentler than it had been in months, "breathe. You did nothing wrong. Absolutely nothing."

Marina looked up at her, her wrinkled hands shaking slightly, her eyes wide and glassy.

Sophia gave a small smile that was warm in its rarity and added, "I should be the one apologizing. I'm sorry I left without saying anything. I wasn't upset with you. I wasn't even upset at home. It was just… something I had to clear up, immediately."

Marina blinked, speechless.

Sophia continued, "Now… about that cupcake. May I still have it?"

Marina's face lit up as if someone had lifted a weight off her chest. She nodded eagerly, her voice catching. "Yes! Of course, ma'am. I'll bring it right away. It's still fresh, I, I kept it in the fridge just in case."

Sophia nodded. "Good. And… I need your help."

Marina straightened, her hands pausing.

"I need to pack," Sophia added. "I'm leaving… soon."

Marina blinked. "Leaving?"

Sophia gave a nod as she began to unbutton her coat, already walking toward her room with certain energy that bordered on excitement.

"Yes," she replied without turning back. "It's urgent."

"Urgent?" Marina reverberated, following behind. "Are you …"

But before she could finish her question, Sophia vanished into her bedroom, her laughter trailing faintly behind her , not loud, not wild, but light. Freeing.

It startled Marina so deeply that she stood frozen in the hallway for a moment longer, blinking at the doorway.

She hadn't heard Sophia laugh like that since… well, never.

As she turned slowly to go retrieve the cupcake, she heard the security door click again.

"Marina," called the guard from the front door, holding something in his hand.

She turned, half-floating from the surreal air of the house. "Yes?"

He walked closer, holding an envelope. "This just arrived. Letter for Ms. Carter."

Marina blinked, took the cream-colored envelope in her hand.

Before she could say anything, Imran stepped into the hallway too, fidgeting with his cap and glancing around as though looking for someone.

"Is she… is she gone?" he asked in a near whisper.

Marina nodded. "Yes. Just now."

Imran gave a breath of relief and then leaned in closer. "She, she smiled."

The guard, still standing nearby, chuckled. "She did. I saw her face when she walked in. First time I've seen that look since… ever."

Marina held the letter to her chest and whispered, "She said she's going somewhere. Urgently."

The men shared a glance.

Imran tilted his head. "Did she say where?"

"No," Marina replied. "But she asked for the cupcake."

Imran chuckled. "Now I've definitely never seen that happen."

"She also asked me to pack her bags."

The guard raised a brow. "Well, that is something."

Imran scratched his head. "I thought if she ever took a trip, it'd be one of those elite places, Maldives, Greece, Bangkok."

"She's never shown any interest in those," Marina replied thoughtfully.

"Well," Imran said with a sly grin, "maybe she is now."

"Hmm," Marina hummed, still clutching the letter. "Maybe…"

None of them could quite figure out what was going on.

The door creaked open to reveal a room that no longer looked like the carefully curated sanctuary of Sophia Carter, it looked like a storm had touched down and spilled every secret it could find.

Her bed was no longer pristine with its ivory duvet tucked in tight folds. Now it was a display of scattered dresses, soft linens, silks, cottons in pale pastels, some half-folded, others abandoned mid-selection. Shoes lined the floor beneath like they were preparing for a performance, and accessories, necklaces, and delicate scarves were draped across the headboard like vines on a forgotten trellis.

Amid the soundless mess sat a peculiar object.

A small wooden box, no bigger than a loaf of bread, sat near the corner of the bed, dark-stained, with brass lining and a little latch that gleamed under the afternoon light. Its surface was worn, faintly engraved with exquisite carvings that had faded from touch and time. It looked… antique. Not just old. Vintage. It had the soul of a secret and the weight of memory.

And for someone who had always favored the latest, the sharpest cut, the newest polish, the minimalist modern, it was strange.

Even stranger to Marina, who now stood at the door with a tray in her hands, holding a steaming mug of coffee and a small plate with the cupcake from the morning.

She took a step in and stopped, her eyes immediately locking onto the box.

She had worked in this house for years, dusted its corners, arranged its flowers, organized Sophia's closets, but she had never seen that box.

It didn't belong. And yet… somehow, it fit. Quietly. Boldly.

She stepped further in, carefully placing the tray on the small table near the reading chair.

Sophia, kneeling at the foot of the bed, rummaging through a lower drawer, looked up and offered a distracted but warm smile.

"Ah, thank you, Marina."

Marina nodded but couldn't hold back. "That box… I've never seen it before."

Sophia paused, glanced at it, then back at Marina. "It was my grandfather's."

That one sentence was enough. It explained everything.

Marina said nothing more about it but kept her gaze on it for a second longer, before stepping closer and rolling up her sleeves. "Alright. Let's get this done."

She began picking up a few light dresses, gently folding them into a suitcase.

"This one?" she asked, holding up a soft lavender wrap dress.

Sophia tilted her head, squinting. "Hmm. No. Too heavy."

Marina picked another, a dark green silk with embroidered cuffs. "This?"

"No. Too dark. Too serious."

Marina laughed. "Well, excuse me, ma'am. I thought we were packing for an elite holiday. A beach, a spa, maybe the Maldives."

Sophia chuckled and shook her head, standing to recheck her toiletry bag. "No Maldives."

"Well then, Paris?"

"No."

"Bangkok?"

Sophia smiled wider, zipping a pouch. "Nope."

"Then where, ma'am?" Marina asked, placing her hands on her hips, half-playful, half-exasperated.

"Willow Creek."

Marina froze.

Her hands paused mid-fold, her brows lifting. "Willow... Creek?"

Sophia nodded casually. "Yes."

"The village?"

Sophia chuckled. "Is there another?"

Marina dropped the dress. "Ma'am, I thought you were escaping to the sea, not returning to the soil!"

Sophia walked past her, grabbing a pair of sandals. "Well, soil is exactly where I need to be."

"But... but that's a small village! Dirt roads! No spas! No gourmet food!"

"That's the charm."

Marina blinked, visibly struggling to process the information. "Are you... alright?"

"I'm better than alright."

Marina gave her a slow, skeptical look but didn't press further.

Just as they were almost done, Sophia's phone buzzed from the dresser. She picked it up, glanced at the screen.

"Nathan," she said aloud.

Then answered. "Yes?"

"Ma'am," Nathan's voice came, smooth but slightly breathless. "Your seat is confirmed. Departure from Penn Station tonight at 8:30. Lancaster by midnight. I've arranged a private car to Willow Creek from there. Names on file, everything's covered."

Sophia smiled to herself. "Thank you, Nathan."

"Are you… really going there?"

"Yes," she replied simply.

There was a beat of silence before he spoke again. "I hope you find what you're looking for."

She didn't answer that. She ended the call and turned to the coffee. Took a sip. Rich. Hot. Perfect.

Then she looked at the cupcake, smiling.

"This is good," she said after a bite. "Very good."

Marina beamed like a child getting praised at school. "Really?"

"Yes. Thank you."

Then, Sophia's gaze drifted to the tray again. She frowned slightly.

"When did this arrive?" Marina followed her eyes and gasped, suddenly remembering.

"Oh! The letter, I forgot to mention it. It just arrived, right before Imran came upstairs."

Sophia nodded slowly. But she didn't reach for it. Not yet. Instead, she finished the cupcake. Then the coffee. Only when the last bag was zipped and the room looked a little more like itself did she finally pick up the envelope.

She walked to the window, broke the seal, unfolded the page and then she read.

"Some roots run so deep, they don't bloom , they anchor. And in doing so, they keep a tree alive even when its branches forget the shape of spring.

We are all creatures of forgetting. You, perhaps more than most. You've made an art of it. But forgetting isn't healing. It's pausing the pain and calling it progress.

You once told someone, maybe yourself , that the silence of Willow Creek haunted you.

But what if it wasn't haunting?

What if it was waiting?

There are places where time folds into itself. The Ridge is one of them. It doesn't age. It remembers. And it hasn't let go of you. Not yet.

When you return, listen. Not with your ears. With your memory.

There are voices buried in its walls. Not the kind you fear. The kind you forgot how to believe. And if you still can't hear them, then open the box. The one you still haven't touched.

You're not running, Sophia. You're circling back. Sometimes, home isn't where you end up.

It's where you begin again."

Sophia read the letter again.

And again.

She didn't fully understand it. Not yet.

The city lights were slowly dissolving into the soft shades of twilight as Sophia Carter sat quietly in the backseat of her car. Her usually unreadable face wore a strange serenity today, not calm, but rather subdued, like a piano key held mid-press, suspended between silence and melody.

Imran, her driver, glanced at her occasionally through the rearview mirror, trying to read her expression , or maybe just hoping to witness it change. But Sophia was far away now, unreachable, locked inside a timeline that no longer belonged to the ticking of clocks.

She didn't speak much throughout the drive. Her hands rested over the armrest, still and poised, her fingers lightly brushing the edge of her phone, but never really gripping it. Her suitcase sat beside her, packed, zipped, and ready. But was she?

The route to the airport was familiar. Too familiar.

But today, it didn't feel like a business trip, or a formal getaway. It felt heavier, like returning to a birthplace. Like walking into a memory. And perhaps that's what it truly was.

Because even before the car pulled into the departure lane, Sophia was no longer in New York. She was twelve again. She was holding her mother's hand.

It was raining that day too , not a heavy rain, but one of those light drizzles that seem more like mist than water that turns breath into smoke and makes every goodbye feel like the end of a movie.

Her mother's hand was warm. Soft, but trembling.

Sophia remembered how tightly she had gripped it, not because she was scared , she wasn't one of those girls , but because her mother's grip had scared her. It felt final. It felt like goodbye.

The entrance to JFK had looked like a palace to her back then , massive, shining, glassy. She remembered looking up at the ceiling and wondering how the world had gotten so big.

Her mother hadn't said much during that drive either. Her words were limited, laced with an artificial cheerfulness that tried too hard to be brave.

"New York is going to be so good for you," she had said with a smile that curved but never reached her eyes. "You'll study in one of the best schools. You'll have opportunities. You'll be unstoppable."

"But what about you?" Sophia had asked, not understanding the unreadable ache in her mother's eyes.

"I'll come back for you. I'll be there before you know it," her mother had whispered, brushing a curl away from Sophia's forehead.

She remembered the way her mother's scarf had shifted slightly as she bent to kiss her forehead, how the scent of sandalwood and old paper had wrapped around her like a memory she'd never forget.

That was the last time she saw her mother.

Sophia's eyes, now staring blankly at the airport's towering glass doors, welled up. But not enough to cry. Not yet. She was still recalling.

After that day, she had been dropped into a different world , into a private hostel, surrounded by unfamiliar faces, tight schedules, grey bedsheets, and cold breakfasts. No one asked her how she felt. No one noticed when she cried in the shower. And no one came to visit.

Weeks passed. Then months. Then years.

Only letters.

She had sent letters herself , timid ones at first, then more desperate with time. But they were never answered. She convinced herself maybe her mother was busy. Maybe the postman was lazy. Maybe the letters got lost.

But deep down, a voice whispered what she didn't want to believe.

Until, six years later, the day she was about to graduate high school, a man appeared at the hostel. He looked older, weary, sunken-eyed. He conveyed a letter, sealed with a wax stamp. No name. Just the handwriting she hadn't seen in years.

She had torn it open in front of him. It said only one thing.

"Forgive me, my daughter. I couldn't keep my promise. I love you more than words can carry. Always."

Her mother had died. And with her, died the last bridge between Sophia and the only home she had ever known.

Back in the present, a soft hum of a suitcase wheel rolling against pavement pulled her from her thoughts.

Imran cleared his throat, gently. "Ma'am… we're here."

Sophia blinked. Once. Twice. Then exhaled slowly and nodded.

She stepped out of the car, adjusting the strap of her handbag. She stood on the departure sidewalk for a moment longer than necessary, her heels tapping softly against the wet concrete as people moved around her like fast-forwarded scenes in a movie she didn't care to watch.

She looked up at the airport signage. She wasn't going to Paris, or Thailand, or any tropical escape. She was going to Willow Creek.

And even though the world called it a village, to her, it had once been a kingdom, her grandfather's kingdom.

She could still see the carved stone arch of The Ridge, nestled on that gentle elevation, overlooking the rows of poppy fields and the old oak trees that lined the outskirts of town. The house wasn't grand in its extravagance, but it was majestic in its roots, in its presence, in its purpose.

People didn't just live in Willow Creek. They belonged there.

And Sophia?

She had once belonged too.

As the trolley carrying her suitcase trailed behind her, she walked toward the entrance.

The automatic doors opened.

And with them, an inaudible promise:

"I'm coming back."

Not just to the land or the house. But to the little girl who still lived in those fields, still clutched that bear in her sleep, still waited for a mother who wouldn't return, and still believed that home wasn't a place, but a feeling.

She glanced at the digital boards. Her flight was on time.

Still early. She had time to sit. Time to think. Time to breathe.

As she found a quiet corner near the large windows overlooking the runway, she sat down slowly and reached into her bag , her fingers brushing against the edge of the last letter.

She didn't read it again. She just held it there, tucked between her fingers like a talisman.

Outside, planes taxied and soared, blinking lights against the now purpling sky. And inside her , something else was finally taking flight.

She didn't know what she was going to find in Willow Creek. Or who. Or whether the person behind the letters would show himself. She didn't even know what she would say if he did.

But she knew one thing. She was no longer running away. She was running towards something.

The airport felt usual, feet tapping on polished tiles, suitcases rolling in unison, soft intercom announcements weaving through the air like elevator music for travelers. But for Sophia Carter, it wasn't sound she was hearing.

It was memory. It was every reverberate of a past that walked beside her now, invisible but weighty.

Her heels clicked against the floor as she made her way through Terminal 4, a large scarf loosely draped around her shoulders. Her face looked composed, as always, sharp eyes, sculpted cheekbones, expression unreadable. But something inside her was untieing with every step.

This wasn't only a terminal. This was a portal. A breath she never finished. A wound that never closed.

It was here, at this very airport, that she had last walked beside her mother, hand in hand, a twelve-year-old girl with pigtails and a heart too small to understand why a smile could feel so sad.

She paused near Gate 29, the same gate they had waited at all those years ago.

Her fingers brushed the cold edge of a nearby chair as if by instinct, and her eyes drifted, unfocused, as a vision began to form again , uninvited but vivid.

She saw herself. Twelve.

Wearing a cream-colored sweater and too-big sneakers. Her hand tightly wrapped in her mother's.

"Do you remember what I said, habit?" her mother had whispered. "If you ever miss me too much, just look up at the moon. That way, no matter where we are, we're looking at the same thing."

Sophia had nodded, trying hard not to cry. She remembered her mother's hands, warm, gentle, but trembling. The way her knuckles turned white when she hugged her too tight. The way her voice cracked when she promised, "I'll come back for you. Soon."

That promise had kept Sophia breathing for years.

But now, standing there, surrounded by strangers and ticketing counters, she felt those words settle in her chest like broken glass. She took a slow step forward.

The boarding signs gleamed, but her mind didn't care for destinations anymore. It was drifting, fast and deep.

She heard a sound, a giggle. Her own. Twelve years old again, hopping around the terminal with curiosity, tugging her mother's scarf and asking about the size of the plane.

The memory slammed into her, leaving her breathless. She turned sharply.

No one was there. Just strangers. Businessmen. Families. Backpackers. But none of them conveyed her laugh.

It had come from inside her head. Her own memory. A hallucination, maybe. But so clear, so real.

She sat down suddenly on the nearest bench, clasping her hands tightly between her knees.

And that's when the voices came. Not loud. Not chaotic. Just… there.

The voice of her grandfather, firm and warm: "A home is not where you live, Sophia. It's where you're remembered."

Her grandmother, soft and tired, brushing Sophia's curls back: "You have your father's eyes, child. And maybe… maybe his fate too. He was too kind for this world. Don't be that kind."

And then, her mother again, barely a whisper: "Be brave. Be brighter than I was allowed to be."

Sophia closed her eyes tightly. And the memories unraveled in full.

The crash came first. The sound of glass shattering. The sickening crunch of metal folding. The scent of burnt rubber and something darker.

She hadn't seen the car flip, but she had felt it.

Her father's voice, deep and rich, had cried out only once before silence swallowed the world.

Then came the hospital.

She had sat in the waiting room, her little fingers interlaced with her grandmother's, as the doctors spoke in low tones.

"He didn't make it," they had said.

And her mother, bruised, bandaged, barely conscious, didn't speak for days after that.

Sophia remembered watching her from a chair by the hospital bed. Machines blinking. Beeping. Wires and tubes like strange vines.

"Mama?" she had whispered once.

Her mother's lips had moved, but no sound came. Life didn't stop. It limped.

Her mother came home , slower, weaker, never quite whole. Her grandmother cooked in silence. Her grandfather sat on the porch and stared too long at the fields.

And one day, her grandmother , who never cried in front of anyone , sat beside Sophia and pulled her into her lap.

"He had your curiosity, too," she said, voice thin. "Your father. Always asking. Always climbing trees."

Sophia looked up. "Did you love him a lot?"

Her grandmother nodded, eyes brimming. "He was my heart. And now... now I see pieces of him in you. I hope... I hope the world's kinder to you than it was to him."

"But what did he do?" Sophia had asked once.

Her grandmother never answered.

Only said, "Something too big for a place this small."

Then came the death that felt quiet.

Her grandmother, who once sang lullabies and made warm ginger tea , died of a silent heart attack. One moment, she was hanging the clothes to dry. The next, she was gone.

Sophia had stood frozen in the doorway, watching the neighbors rush in.

She never saw her grandfather cry. But he stopped speaking for days.

And when her mother began packing suitcases one morning, he didn't help. He didn't even look at Sophia when she hugged him goodbye.

He only turned away, as if saying, I can't lose you too.

Then came New York.

The hostel. The years of loneliness.

And finally, the letter from the old man who knocked on the gate of her school the day she turned eighteen.

Her grandfather had died two years earlier. No letter. No goodbye.

She had officially become an orphan without being told.

And then, the second blow. The one she thought her heart wouldn't survive. The letter in her mother's handwriting.

Folded. Carefully written.

"I didn't want you to watch me die, habibti. I wanted you to grow. To become someone, I never could. You were my only good decision. I'm sorry I couldn't wait for you."

Sophia opened her eyes. Back in the airport now.

A baby was crying somewhere. A couple was laughing. A luggage cart rolled too fast and knocked into a bench.

Life , ordinary, noisy, ongoing , swirled around her.

But inside? She was still holding that twelve-year-old girl.

The one who had lost everyone. The one who didn't understand why everyone she loved either left or died. The one who learned to be strong not because she was brave, but because she had no one else. She exhaled, long and slow.

And finally stood up. Wiped the corners of her eyes , though they weren't wet.

Straightened her coat. She wasn't here for closure. She was here to confront the past.

To walk through its silence. To remember on her own terms. And maybe, to forgive.

CHAPTER 6: THE LONG WAITED REVISIT

The wheels rolled onto the countryside highway just as the sun began to stretch its golden limbs across the sky. It had been a quiet landing, no press, no staff, no eyes watching her. That, in itself, had felt foreign. But freeing.

Sophia Carter stood outside the small Lancaster station terminal, her luggage beside her, the air around her carrying the kind of crisp scent that can only be found outside city walls, part soil, part grass, part air that hadn't been breathed a million times before.

The private car her assistant had booked for her arrived in a sputter of engine and a cheerfulness so loud it made the pigeons nearby scatter.

It wasn't sleek or glossy like her usual rides.

It was a deep blue hatchback, probably a decade old, with chipped paint near the bumper and a dreamcatcher swinging from the rearview mirror. The man behind the wheel waved before even fully parking.

He was in his late sixties, with a faded baseball cap, sun-darkened skin, and a smile so wide it creased the corners of his eyes like folded paper.

"You must be Miss Sophia! Carter, right?" he called, stepping out and tipping his cap as if she were royalty returning from exile. "I'm Harlen. Harlen Wyatt. Folks call me Hally. Welcome back to Willow Creek, young lady!"

Sophia blinked, nodded, and smiled faintly. "Thank you."

"I'd shake your hand proper," he added with a wink, "but these old fingers are covered in engine grease, and I doubt your nice coat would survive it."

Sophia chuckled, surprisingly at ease already. "I appreciate the consideration."

He took her bag and heaved it into the backseat with a grunt, muttering to himself about how 'luggage these days weigh like secrets people forget to confess.'

Once they were both inside the car, and the doors were shut, he started the engine , which coughed to life after a moment's hesitation , and pulled out onto the winding road leading to Willow Creek.

And then, Harlen started talking.

And didn't stop.

"You know, miss," he said, eyes crinkled at the edges as he glanced at her through the mirror, "you did the right thing coming here. All these city folk, always running to other countries, beaches, Bali, Lord-knows-where. What they don't know is that peace ain't sold by airlines. It's right here, between cornfields and chapel bells."

Sophia smiled but kept her gaze on the road outside.

"It's been a while since I came back," she offered softly.

He gave a knowing nod. "Ah, that's the thing with roots. You don't always see 'em, but they know when you're coming back. You'll see , Willow Creek remembers."

They passed endless stretches of greenery, some wild, some tamed into tidy little farms. The horizon yawned wide and far, dotted by windmills and old barns with peeling paint that looked more charming than shabby in the soft light.

"You ever see a dawn like this in New York?" Harlen continued, gesturing grandly out the windshield. "Out there, the sun shows up like it's late for work. Here? It strolls in. Like it's got nowhere else it needs to be but home."

Sophia didn't speak, but her heart was listening.

She let her window down slightly, and the breeze conveyed in the scent of hay, of flowers that hadn't been arranged but still bloomed beautifully.

Harlen glanced over, then chuckled. "You're not mindin' my talkin', are ya?"

"No," she said, smiling. "Actually… I'm grateful for it."

He beamed. "Well, that's rare. Most these days just bury their heads in phones and pretend the driver don't exist."

Sophia rested her head lightly against the window, eyes drinking in the unfolding canvas of her childhood.

This was a return. It was an arrival. And everything looked smaller. Not in a disappointing way. Just in the way that time shrinks places you once thought were bigger than life. She felt like both a stranger and a native.

Like time had folded, and she had fallen through its seam.

"I used to run along this path," she murmured, more to herself than anyone.

"I bet you did," Harlen said, grinning. "Miss, we remember everything here. Even what we pretend we forgot."

There was a silence that followed. But not empty.

It was full. Of fields. Of nostalgia. Of moments lost in years and suddenly found again like pennies in an old coat.

Finally, as they neared the edge of the village, Harlen pointed toward a small slope.

"There," he said.

And in the distance, just barely visible behind a line of oaks and lilacs, stood a vintage hotel.

Its roof was slate-gray, windows tall, and porch seemed proud and welcoming. Sophia leaned forward slightly, breath caught somewhere between awe and ache.

She was almost home.

The morning in Willow Creek unfolded like a silk scarf slipping off a windowsill, soft, unhurried, untouched by the frenzy of modern hours. The air was scented with freshly upturned earth and something faintly citrusy, like early bloom. The sun climbed slow and gentle, emitting long shadows from trees that had stood for generations.

Sophia Carter stepped out of the small inn where she'd rested the night before, her breath caught somewhere between purpose and confusion. She wore a loose white shirt tucked lazily into high-waisted cotton trousers; her feet slipped into flat sandals that didn't match the image most people had of her. A small brown leather bag slung over one shoulder. Her hair, usually twisted into sharp professionalism, was pulled back into a low, hasty ponytail, strands slipping free to frame her face.

She didn't look like the Sophia Carter who once ruled over high-rises and headlines. She looked like someone softer. Searching.

She walked with intention, but with nowhere precise to go. She had asked three people already, the tea-seller outside the inn, the postman pushing his rusty cycle, and a mother holding her toddler outside a sweets shop, all of them had given her half-answers, incomplete directions, or blank stares.

"The Ridge?" the postman had asked, scratching his head. "Well, miss, do you mean the actual ridge or the Ridge house?"

Both, she had thought. But she couldn't quite explain it. It wasn't on Google Maps. There was no signboard. There was no Uber, no GPS pin, no taxi lane. It was memory she was chasing. Not a location.

She kept walking.

The sun had grown warmer now, and sweat shimmered like dew on her skin. The fabric of her shirt stuck slightly to her back, and her shoulders gleamed under the light like delicate porcelain brushed with moisture.

She'd stopped by every cart and small vehicle she came across , an old scooter, a goods rickshaw, even a man with a bicycle cart loaded with crates of mangoes. She didn't mind the awkward stares or the villagers whispering to each other behind her back.

If anything, she was grateful they didn't know who she was. It allowed her to be… anonymous.

Normal. Human

Her breath was beginning to labor just slightly when she spotted it. Across the bend of the unpaved path, past a cluster of jasmine bushes, a horse stood.

Not just any horse.

But a fine white stallion, tall, powerful, with a mane like silk threads caught in the morning wind. Its coat was almost shimmering under the rising sun, each muscle beneath it outlined in subtle grace. The kind of horse you don't just see , you remember.

Sophia stopped walking. Her bag slipped slightly on her shoulder as her feet paused in the soft dirt. The scene was so surreal, it made her heart slow.

The horse was tethered to a post beside a narrow wooden fence, under the shade of a neem tree. It stood still, almost regal, its large eyes scanning the world with calm patience.

Sophia took a small step forward, then another, hesitant, respectful. She didn't speak. She didn't need to. The horse turned its head slightly, ears flicking in her direction.

And then, for no reason she could explain, she reached out her hand. Not fully. Just a little. As if offering peace.

She didn't want to ride it.

She didn't want to own it.

She just wanted to touch something that hadn't been trained by cities, dressed in polish, or drowned in ambition. Something real. The horse didn't flinch. It didn't move away.

It simply stood there.

And Sophia stepped closer, her fingers brushing the edge of the fence. She leaned in and gently laid her hand on the horse's neck, caressing its smooth, warm skin.

For a few seconds, there was no noise. No village. Nostalgia hitting her .

Just this, the softness of a beast too beautiful to be ignored, and the ache in her chest that told her she had spent too many years not touching anything this alive.

The breeze lifted, catching strands of her hair and sweeping the heat from her skin.

She let out a breath she didn't realize she'd been holding. And then, for the first time since she had landed, she smiled.

Not for anyone.

Not for the camera.

Not even for herself.

She smiled because, somehow, the universe had given her a moment, still and unexpected, where beauty wasn't decorated. It just was.

The sun had crept higher into the sky, but the morning air in Willow Creek still held the cool whisper of dew. Sophia Carter had barely walked ten paces from the white horse when something shifted in her periphery.

A rustle.

A breath.

A shadow.

Her eyes turned.

And there, like a painting unveiled slowly, stood another horse, dark as ink, glossy and regal, the contrast of its midnight coat glowing against the golden meadow light. Its main swayed with the breeze, thick and long, as if the wind itself admired it too much to resist a caress.

Sophia stopped. For a moment, her breath hitched. Because now it made sense.

They were a pair. Black and white. Night and dawn. Standing together like some old fairytale made real.

The symmetry of them, the hushed authority, the sheer elegance of their presence, it gripped her like a memory from a story she'd never heard but always known. She stepped toward them without a second thought, her eyes shimmering in the sunlight.

It wasn't just admiration. It was... enchantment. It brought severe nostalgia to her mind along with the flood of memories because last time she had seen such beautiful horses was fifteen years back when she went on a walk with her grandpa and admired those beautiful beasts from a distance.

As she approached, her steps slowed, her gaze lowered to the ground near the horses' legs, and that's when she saw him.

A man. Kneeling.

His back slightly turned, shoulder brushing the black horse's side as he worked on something by the saddle. A simple grey shirt hugged his broad shoulders, sleeves rolled to the elbows, tan forearms strong and steady, his posture absorbed, confident, quiet. He looked like someone who belonged to the earth, not in dirt, but in rhythm.

She stood there for a few moments, unsure what to say, unsure why her heart had suddenly begun tapping so audibly.

But then, she spoke.

"Hey," she called gently, voice not quite loud, but clear.

He didn't look up.

"Excuse me?" she tried again, a little firmer this time.

His head turned slightly, just enough that she caught a glimpse of the sharp cut of his jawline, the lazy sweep of stubble, and the faint curve of a smirk.

"Yes?" he replied, voice smooth, relaxed, a deep manly voice though.

"I was wondering…" She hesitated for a beat. "How much would you charge for a ride?"

His fingers paused mid-motion. He turned his head further this time, just enough for her to see the side of his face.

"Sorry?" he asked, as if amused.

"I asked," she said, brushing a stray hair from her forehead and folding her arms, "how much would a ride cost? On one of your horses."

He let out a breathy laugh then, not mocking, just surprised. Straightening slowly, he turned to face her. And the full picture hit her like a second sunrise.

Tall. Windswept hair tucked beneath a loose hood. A face that didn't need explanation, confident but soft in its detail. Eyes a shade too unreadable for green, too warm for grey.

He looked at her, not through her, not around her, at her.

A pause followed. Then he named an amount. Something ridiculous. Something no sane local would charge for a five-minute ride through the outskirts of Willow Creek but Sophia never understood that.

She blinked. Once. Then she reached into her bag, pulled out a wallet, and handed him the exact amount in cash. Without blinking. Without asking a single follow-up question. He looked down at the notes, then up at her, brows arched.

"You're serious?"

"I wouldn't be handing you money otherwise," she replied, and with a breath of boldness that surprised even herself, she stepped closer to the white horse, placed a gentle hand on its neck, and swung one leg over the saddle with the elegance of someone who clearly hadn't ridden in years, but knew how to pretend she had.

The man stared. A beat passed. Then another. "You didn't even told me where should I take you," he finally said, a low chuckle in his voice.

"I don't need to," she said, her tone light, her grip steady on the reins. "You'll figure it out soon."

He laughed again, deeper this time, clearly taken off-guard. "You didn't ask if these horses were even for riding. Or if they were trained."

"They're trained," she said, running a hand through the white horse's mane. "Oh, aren't they for the transportation purpose? I thought they are.."

He shook his head, stepping to his own horse , the dark one , with a look of half disbelief, half admiration.

"You do this often? Wander into strangers' mornings and throw money at them for mystery rides?"

She just stared at him for a while, thinking he was just another yapping driver, or a sibling of the one she got to Willow Creek with, yes, Hallen.

He mounted his horse in one fluid motion, the black stallion responding instantly with a proud toss of its head.

They rode in silence at first, a soft, clopping duet of hooves against earth, as the fields on either side opened like arms welcoming her back home. The path curved through quiet meadows, sprinkled with marigolds and daisies, distant cows grazing lazily under old trees. Butterflies danced in and out of the sunlight like scattered gold.

"You're not from here," he said finally, emitting her a sideways glance.

"I used to be," she replied.

"And now?"

She shrugged. "Now I'm figuring it out."

"I like that."

She turned to him. "You don't even know what I mean."

"That's why I like it," he said, that same half-smile curling on his lips again. "Most people want to be understood before they've figured out themselves."

Sophia blinked. He was not as stupid as she thought him to be. The breeze picked up, tugging at the hem of her shirt. She felt it then, that glimmer. That danger wrapped in ease. That chemistry that isn't declared or sought, just felt.

She cleared her throat. "So… do you always name absurd prices for horse rides?"

He grinned. "Only when I know someone can afford it."

She laughed. "So I look like someone who can?"

"You look like someone who doesn't need to ask."

That caught her off guard. She looked away, suddenly flustered.

They rode further, winding between trees, past an old wooden gate that looked like it belonged in a storybook. Birds chirped overhead. Somewhere in the distance, a bell rang faintly, maybe from the chapel, maybe from a passing cart.

"So what's your name?" she asked, turning back to him.

He smiled but didn't answer immediately.

"What would you like it to be?" he replied, eyes gleaming with mischief.

She scoffed. "Seriously?"

"Alright," he said, relenting. "It's Ethan."

"Ethan …"

"And you, Miss Doesn't Ask Questions?"

She paused. Then she looked at him.

"Sophia," she said. "Just Sophia."

He didn't press for a last name. She was grateful for that.

And the ride continued with the horse hooves reverberating against the path, trees dancing above, the sun pouring light like syrup over the road. The horses moved slowly now, their pace relaxed beneath the swishing canopy of tall trees. Willow Creek's air had grown warmer with the rising sun, but the shade of the woods kept the world cool and easy, like an early chapter in a story that hadn't quite decided what genre it belonged to yet.

Ethan rode a little ahead, occasionally tossing glances over his shoulder to check on Sophia. His wide-brimmed cowboy hat tilted slightly forward, emitting a soft shadow over his eyes, but not enough to hide the way they gleaned when he smiled.

Sophia, sitting atop the white horse with remarkable ease, had her back straight, her gaze steady, her presence poised, as it always was. Her shirt was dusted slightly with the road's trail, her hair whipped gently by the breeze, and yet, somehow, she still managed to look like she belonged on a magazine cover. If not for the dusty boots and the countryside silence, one might've mistaken her for an actress playing "undercover country girl."

But here, there was no cover. No scripts. Only questions.

"So… you never said where you were headed," Ethan finally said, his voice casual, his posture loose in the saddle.

"I did," Sophia replied, her tone calm, clipped. "The Ridge."

He looked back again, brows raised. "You mean the actual ridge? Like, up near the forest line?"

"No. The Ridge house."

Ethan pulled the reins slightly and slowed his horse to ride beside her.

"The Ridge house?" he repeated followed by a long pause. "Now that's a name I haven't heard in a long while. Nobody calls it that anymore. Folks just refer to it as the old Carter estate."

Her fingers tightened subtly around the reins. He didn't notice, or pretended not to.

"I was trying to get there earlier," she said. "Stopped half the village, asked every driver or cart I could find. Nobody seemed to know what I was talking about."

Ethan squinted toward the horizon. "That sounds about right."

"Why?"

"Because most people around here are either too young to remember or too old to drive."

That made her glance at him, just for a second. He caught it.

He chuckled. "So… how'd you know about it? The Ridge, I mean."

She blinked. Paused.

"I just… know," she said.

Ethan tilted his head. "You just know?"

"Yes."

"That's oddly vague."

"I suppose."

"You're not great at answering questions, are you?"

"I'm not required to be," she said coolly.

He laughed, a rich, throaty sound, deep enough to vibrate the silence of the trail.

"Well, that's fair," he said. "But you don't look like someone who's here by accident. You ride like you've done this before."

"I have."

"Recently?"

She shook her head. "No."

"City girl?"

"Yes."

"New York?"

Another glance.

He nodded. "You've got the eyes for it."

"I beg your pardon?"

He grinned. "City people have this look. Like they're carrying ten years of to-do lists in their pockets."

Sophia smirked or it was just a little glint. "Maybe I am."

"Well," Ethan said, patting the side of his horse, "you wear it well. But you don't walk like someone who's running from the city. You walk like someone who's… finding something."

She looked away. That was dangerous territory.

He seemed to realize it too, because he eased the reins again, letting silence settle for a moment before speaking again, lighter this time.

"So, Sophia, that's your name, right?"

"Yes."

"Just Sophia?"

"That's what I said."

"Right. Sorry. My interrogation mode's a little rusty."

She didn't reply.

He waited for another beat. Then, more gently: "So, what brings you to the Ridge? If you don't mind me asking."

She hesitated. Felt the answer press against her lips. Then swallowed it.

"I just wanted to see it," she said simply. "It's been a long time."

Ethan studied her side profile, the way her lashes dropped, the way her jaw clenched slightly before relaxing again.

"You knew someone who lived there?" he tried again.

Sophia turned slightly, her eyes narrowed, not hostile, but defensive.

"Do all the drivers here ask this many questions?"

Ethan blinked. Then he grinned. A wide, lopsided, helpless grin. "Driver?" he repeated.

She didn't respond.

He touched his hat, tipping it like a man humoring royalty. "Ma'am, I was just tending to my horses when a stranger walked up, threw money at me, and climbed on like she was going into battle."

Sophia blinked. "You're not a driver?"

He laughed. "God, no. I'm a carpenter."

Now it was her turn to be stunned.

"But… you said yes."

"You didn't give me much of a choice."

She narrowed her eyes. "You quoted a price."

"A ridiculous one. As a joke."

"And I paid it."

"And that's when I realized either you were out of your mind, or I was about to have the most interesting morning of my year."

Sophia pressed her lips together, unable to tell if she was amused, embarrassed, or, strangely, intrigued.

Ethan leaned back slightly in the saddle, letting his horse slow. "So, now that we've established that I'm not your chauffeur, and you're not just another lost tourist… who are you really?"

She stared at him. Then back at the path.

Then said quietly, "Well, yes someone lived there but no longer important."

He tilted his head. "See, I don't believe that."

She didn't answer. Didn't need to. Because in her silence, in her carefully composed avoidance, Ethan saw the cracks. The weight. The reluctance to be seen.

But he didn't press further. Not yet. Instead, he smiled gently and let the silence breathe.

And Sophia, surprisingly, didn't mind.

Because in all the years she'd spent dodging questions, this was the first time someone had asked and stayed… not because they were entitled to the answer.

But because they were curious about her.

The path had narrowed as they rode, the trees around them thickening like ancient sentinels who had seen everything. The air served as a portrayal with the scent of fresh pine and damp earth, the rustle of leaves beneath the horses' hooves. The world outside was still and waiting, as if holding its breath for what was about to come.

Sophia rode ahead, her focus fixed on the road that curved and twisted toward the familiar figure that rose in the distance, The Ridge. She had dreamed of it, wished for it, but never fully understood how deeply it had rooted itself in her heart.

It wasn't just the house. It was everything. The trees. The hills. The dirt beneath her boots. The air that had once kissed her cheeks like it owned her. Her grandfather's legacy was engraved into the land, into the very soil beneath her, and it was here, at this threshold, where her past had taken its first breaths.

And now, it was her return.

She didn't realize how much she had missed this place until her horse began to gallop faster, instinctively moving closer to the old stone gates that creaked slightly in the wind.

Behind her, Ethan kept his distance, allowing her space, but his eyes never left her. He wasn't watching the gate, the fields, or even the horses. His focus was on her.

Her steady posture. Her determined pace. The way she seemed to command the world around her even when her emotions were tangled like the vines around The Ridge.

Her face, calm yet distant. Strict, yet calm. Like a storm that had swallowed all chaos and turned it into something beautiful. It was a strange thing, watching a woman so composed, so powerful, yet holding something inside her, a quiet ache that only those who had seen too much could carry.

And in that moment, as she leaned forward, pushing the reins with more urgency, he saw it.

Her lips were slightly parted, and the wind played with her hair. But what captivated him wasn't just her beauty.

It was the nonchalant strength that radiated from her, a strength that wasn't born from confrontation but from silence. From the kind of sadness only the deep, quiet places in the world could understand.

Her eyes. Her eyes that never seemed to rest, always searching, always guarding. The way she looked like someone who had been carrying the world on her shoulders for years, and yet still stood tall.

Ethan couldn't help but wonder what it was that weighed so heavily on her heart. She slowed her horse as they reached the edge of the Ridge, her body stiffening as the gate came into full view.

There it was.

Her heart skipped a beat. Sophia stopped. She didn't know why. She hadn't meant to. But her body had acted without her mind's permission. She could feel her chest tighten, her breath catch in her throat.

For a moment, she couldn't move. Her eyes locked onto the door. The old wooden door with the intricate carvings. The door that she once knew like the back of her hand. The door that had seen the start and end of everything.

And then, in one sudden motion, she dismounted the horse. Her feet hit the ground with a thud as if the earth had called her home.

She wasn't in control anymore. Her body was shaking. Her hands were trembling. Her throat felt tight. Her heart was pounding so loudly it filled her ears.

She wanted to say something, anything, but nothing came. Instead, she just covered her mouth, her fingers digging into her skin, trying to hold herself together.

But the tears, they came. And they didn't ask for permission.

Sophia's body trembled as she knelt, the ground beneath her legs feeling colder than it had ever been before. Her hands shook violently. Her breath hitched, and she let out a quiet sob, her shoulders trembling with the weight of everything she had buried in this place.

She could feel it all now. The loss. The abandonment. The weight of promises unkept. And worse, the realization that she had abandoned herself.

No, Sophia Carter can't cry! She never did! Oh God, not at least in front of a stranger she just met a few minutes ago! But, she had no control on herself anymore. She was not in her senses anymore and so she let it happen.

Ethan watched her, the air around him heavy with unsaid realizations. He didn't rush to her. He didn't move.

He let her breathe. Let her break down in whatever way she needed to.

For the first time since they had met, he didn't try to fix anything. He just watched. And his heart tightened, too, because he could see it. Her pain. Her loss. Her quiet suffering that she hadn't let anyone see until now. He dismounted slowly, walking toward her with a calmness that almost didn't belong.

But something in his chest made him stay steady. He knelt beside her, not touching her, but close enough that she could feel the warmth of his presence.

Sophia didn't look at him. She didn't need to. Her head was down, her face hidden behind her hands.

And yet, there he was. Watching her fall apart. Her breath came in ragged gasps, her shoulders trembling harder. And then, in a voice softer than any breath, Ethan spoke.

"You don't have to be strong all the time."

Sophia's head snapped up, her tear-streaked face turning toward him, her eyes wide, filled with disbelief and exhaustion.

"I'm not strong," she whispered.

Ethan smiled softly. "You're more than strong. You just haven't let anyone in to see the rest of you."

Sophia stared at him, a slight glint of surprise flashing across her features.

"Why… are you still here?" she asked, her voice breaking slightly.

He tilted his head. "Because you're not alone."

She shook her head, her tears still falling freely, mixing with the dust beneath her knees.

"But I've always been alone."

Ethan didn't respond with words. Instead, he reached out slowly, gently, and placed a hand on her shoulder. He didn't force her to look at him. He didn't demand anything. He just offered his presence.

"Perhaps, you always had your people, they were just afraid to show up or perhaps you were afraid of showing up to them!"

And Sophia felt something warm, something soft, slide over her soul. She wasn't sure what it was. But it felt like healing. It felt like acceptance. And it felt like someone seeing her.

Just… seeing her.

For who she was.

Without judgement.

Without expectations.

"Do you want to go inside?" he asked, his voice tender.

Sophia didn't speak. She nodded.

Ethan helped her to her feet, standing beside her as they walked slowly toward the house. Finally, Sophia didn't feel like an outsider, she felt like she had come home.

CHAPTER 7: FROM MEMORIES TO REALITY

The once-proud structure of the Carter estate looked older now , not broken, not defeated, but silently surrendered to time. Vines crept up the stone pillars like veins in aging hands. Wooden frames wore the faded elegance of things once polished. The front door screeched like a familiar voice clearing its throat after years of silence.

Sophia didn't say a word as she stepped inside. Ethan, walking a few respectful steps behind, stayed silent too. The light was entering inside after being filtered through the stained windows in shafts of golden dust. Everything smelt of history like, aged wood, like stillness, like old promises.

It was a different silence than the one she was used to. This wasn't the silence of boardrooms or apartment suites. This silence had presence. It knew her name.

Sophia's footsteps reverberated as she crossed the threshold, the floor groaning under her body mass as if recognizing her return. She stood in the wide foyer for a moment taking it all in.

There were no words in her vocabulary for this.

So she didn't try. She just… walked.

From one room to the next, like a ghost slipping back into the fabric of an old life.

The parlor was stripped nearly bare. The long window she used to sit by with a book was fogged now, the seat below it bare wood and dust. Where once settled polished sepia shelves, only a few tilted wooden planks remained, some bent, some empty.

Ethan remained behind her, saying nothing. He didn't ask. Didn't interrupt. He simply followed, not as a guide, not as an intruder, but as someone who knew presence mattered more than speech.

Sophia stepped into the old living area; the fireplace still intact though worn. The walls here had faded to a pale sepia tone. Her shoes crunched on a layer of fallen paint chips. She stood still.

Then slowly, her fingers brushed against the stone mantel, and a whisper slipped out of her mouth.

"This was where he used to…"

She stopped.

Ethan, who had stepped halfway into the room, gently completed the sentence, "Warm his hands every winter morning?"

She turned sharply, shooting a stare at him, startled.

He met her eyes calmly, not smug, not too soft. Just… knowing. As if it had been a guess. A lucky guess.

Sophia looked away again. She didn't explain. She never explained.

They moved again.

Into the corridor that once led to her grandfather's study.

It was mostly empty now, the shelves stripped, the big desk gone. Only a single chair sat in the corner, her grandfather's bed still there in the next room, untouched and covered in an old beige sheet.

She paused in the doorway of that bedroom, hand lightly resting on the frame. Her voice came again, breathy and small.

"This room always smelled like…"

Again, she couldn't finish. Ethan didn't rush it. He stood a few steps behind.

Then said gently, "Like the pages of books that have waited too long to be read."

Sophia's eyes shot up to him again.

This time, he was already looking at her. Their gazes locked for a second too long. And in that second, he saw something he hadn't seen on her face all day, surprise, softness, and the faint shimmer of acknowledgment.

She blinked first. He looked away. They moved on. Down the hall, into the sunroom.

The air here was warmer. The windows had yellowed slightly, catching the sun like old photographs. A single armchair , her grandmother's , still sat in the corner, worn and sagging.

Sophia stopped in front of it. Her fingers hovered just above the fabric. She didn't touch it.

Not yet.

"She used to sit here after lunch," she murmured. Her eyes were distant. "And knit. She was terrible at it. Everything came out crooked." She smiled faintly, a rare thing. And then, under her breath, "But she always said…"

Ethan, quieter than ever, barely above a whisper, said, "'Imperfect threads still make warm things.'"

Sophia turned to him, slowly.

He hadn't meant to say it out loud. And the look in his eyes betrayed that.

She stared at him. Not hostile, not accusatory.

But cautious. "How do you…?"

He straightened slightly. "I just guessed. Sorry, if that was …"

She stepped back, as if pulled by gravity. "You keep… guessing right."

"I know," he said, and looked down for the first time. "It's just … sometimes when people remember the same kind of loss… the words find themselves."

She didn't respond. Didn't argue. But she didn't walk away either. Together, they continued, room by room, down hallways that had shrunk since her childhood but still conveyed the shadows of memory.

She paused by a set of old wind chimes, now tangled and rusted.

He watched her eyes. Watched how they gleamed at each corner, how her fingers trembled near certain objects. It wasn't grief. It was recognition. It was the heart trying to recall how it once beat in a place like this.

They reached the last room a smaller chamber off the kitchen, once her childhood bedroom. It was empty now, save for a crooked mirror and a broken trunk.

Sophia stepped inside. This time, she dropped to her knees, fingers grazing the floor. There was a small etching on one of the floorboards, a heart with the letters S.C. and G.C.

Her initials. And her grandfather's. Her chest tightened. She didn't cry. But she couldn't breathe right either.

Ethan stood in the doorway, not stepping in. A few moments later, he added, "Seems like you visited this place after so long, but not only like someone you knew lived here, instead people dear to you did."

She looked up at him. And this time, her voice wasn't defensive. It wasn't distant. It was curious. She had been ignoring him just as a stranger but how could she? Sophia Carter never left any space for suspicions or strangers to take up. "How do you know what to say?"

He paused. Then answered honestly.

"I don't. I just… try."

Sophia sat back, legs crossed now, her hand resting gently on her chest.

"This place," she said, her voice a whisper, "it never let me go."

Ethan nodded. "Some homes don't."

There was silence again. But this one didn't ache. It pulsed with something else. Familiarity, and perhaps the initial stages of trust.

The air around her felt too emotionally burdened. The silence too loud. The house, for a few rare seconds, no longer pulled at her thoughts, because everything in her focus now was alive. Too alive. Breathing. Watching her.

She had just returned from kneeling on the floorboards of her old bedroom, where her initials were carved like a ghost of her younger self whispering from the wood. Her throat had tightened, her body trembled, only slightly, but it was enough for her to draw in a breath and quickly, almost violently, wipe her face.

It took her less than a second. A sweep of the wrist. A lift of her chin. Shoulders squared.

The transformation was almost flawless.

Almost.

But not to him.

She turned abruptly, catching Ethan still standing a few feet away near the doorway, his eyes still resting softly on her.

And maybe that's what made her snap. She wasn't used to being seen , especially not like this.

"Why are you still here?" she asked, her voice sharpened to steel, the calmness in it betrayed only by the slight crack at the very end.

Ethan didn't move. He tilted his head slightly, the familiar, infuriating half-grin curling on his lips.

"Well," he said, as if it were the most obvious thing in the world, "I only take round-trip travelers. No fun leaving my passengers stranded in strange old houses."

She blinked. For a moment, she didn't even understand. Then she remembered, the ridiculous fare she had paid for the horse ride, and how she had mistaken him for a local rider.

She folded her arms.

"You can go now," she said. "I'm not stranded. I can find my way back."

He took a step forward, still not crossing the invisible line between them.

"It's not close," he said quietly. "And it'll be dark soon. It's not safe."

"You don't need to worry about me," she snapped.

But her words weren't even halfway through before she felt something she had never expected.

His hand on her arm. Not forceful. But firm.

She gasped, not out of pain, but shock. She turned. And he pulled her closer. Just a step. Just enough. And his eyes, which were always calm, always filled with something unreadable, were now different.

There was fire in them. A kind of low, burning intensity that made her stomach twist.

"Why are you so afraid of crying in front of someone?" he asked, voice low, deep, but pulsing with something angry. "Why are you so concerned about holding onto this, this damn performance, instead of just being a person?"

Sophia froze. Her breath caught in her chest.

"You think it makes you strong, keeping it all in?" he continued, still close. His face barely a breath away from hers. "That silence makes you powerful? It doesn't. It makes you bleed in places no one can see. And I can see it."

Her heart pounded.

"I can sense it," he said, softer now, but no less fierce. "You've got no one to cry in front of. I get it. But it doesn't mean you're not allowed to. It doesn't mean you can't."

Sophia didn't speak. She couldn't.

No one had ever spoken to her like that. No one had ever dared to come this close. Not physically. Not emotionally. She had spent years perfecting the art of being untouchable.

And here he was , not just touching her wrist, but cutting through her defenses like they weren't even there. He stared into her eyes, searching, pushing, waiting.

Then something shifted in his jaw. He exhaled, his shoulders stiff. And in one sharp movement, he let go of her arm and turned away, the fire in him now clenched into his fists.

He walked toward the door. Paused at the threshold. And without turning back, he said, quieter now, but still every syllable seething with something primal:

"I'll wait outside. Take your time."

And then… he left. The door creaked. The reverberate of his boots softened with distance.

And Sophia? She stood there. Motionless.

Her skin still tingled where his fingers had gripped her. Her breath came in small, staggered exhales. She blinked slowly. Still trying to comprehend what had just happened. Not because it was loud. But because it wasn't. It was intimate. And raw. And honest. Too honest.

Sophia Carter had faced boardrooms, politicians, analysts, investors. She'd stood before thousands, spoken into microphones, faced down scandal, betrayal, abandonment.

But no one, no one, had ever confronted her like this. Not with cruelty. But with concern. Not with command. But with care. And now, the silence in the room was different. It didn't sound like abandonment. It sounded like someone left… but waited.

Outside, beyond the door, the air stirred with the sounds of the village. A few birds. A low breeze. The occasional crackle of distant leaves.

But inside, she stood still, the walls of The Ridge listening.

And somewhere deep within her, something that she hadn't touched in years, finally whispered back.

Why did he say all that?

The question reverberated in Sophia's mind like a bell still ringing long after its chime. She paced slowly across the warped wooden floor of The Ridge, her steps soft but uncertain, as though the house itself might judge her for her thoughts. Her fingers occasionally brushed the dust-lined walls, not for balance, not to steady herself, but to remember that she was still here. Still present. Still holding the shape of someone strong.

But inside, she was anything but. Why did he say all that?

Why did Ethan, a man who had only known her for a breath of time, look at her and speak those words as if he had traced the exact contours of her silence for years?

Did she look that transparent?

Did she truly appear like someone faking strength?

Was her armor visible for what it was, not steel, but carefully painted glass?

She had spent so many years becoming Sophia Carter; the invincible, composed, untouchable Sophia Carter that she never stopped to imagine anyone might actually see through it. That someone might dare to.

And yet, he had. In one breath.

In one grip of her arm, one flash of fire in his voice, one plea she hadn't asked for but couldn't ignore.

She sank slowly onto the edge of the wooden staircase, her arms wrapped around herself, her body smaller than she'd ever allowed it to be in front of anyone. Her hands twisted into the fabric of her sleeves, and her eyes stared down at the dust-covered step as if the answer might be hiding in its cracks.

Was he right?

Was it that obvious?

Did Marina see it, too?

All those years Marina had watched her skip breakfast, bury exhaustion beneath lipstick and tailored coats, did she guess? Did she know?

And Nathan, with his professional nods, his diligent silence, did he ever leave the office shaking his head, thinking: She's not okay?

Even Imran. Even the guard downstairs. Even the doorman who opened her office building every day. Were they all pretending not to see what Ethan had the audacity to speak aloud?

The realization made her stomach twist. Was she a facade?

A well-tailored performance so over-rehearsed it had started leaking between the seams?

Her head dropped. Her eyes closed. She wanted to scream, but her throat wouldn't obey. And still, beneath it all , buried in the shame, the shock, the confusion , was something else.

Something softer. Relief.

Because for once, just once, someone had looked past the silence. Past the hard lines. Past the glint of steel, she wore around her as if it were skin. And they had said: You don't have to do this alone.

Even if it came as a storm. Even if it came from a man who smiled too easily and joked like the world wasn't burning. Even if it came from someone she didn't trust, not yet. He had seen her.

And that... terrified her more than anything else.

Hours passed and when she stepped out into the fading light, the air felt unusually still, not empty, but heavy, like a sad lofi song only she could hear. If there was music, it was that of flapping wings of birds heading home, the rustle of dry leaves under the wind's breath, and the almost imperceptible hum of a day slipping into dusk.

It felt like a sad song was playing all around her. But no orchestra performed. Just the soft chord of a day ending at a place she once called her own.

Her own.

She almost laughed at the idea. The Ridge didn't feel like hers anymore. Not fully. Not like it had when she'd chased butterflies through its corridors or curled up on its porch during spring rains. But the land remembered her. The silence did. And so, too, did her heart in rebellion.

She walked forward, the dirt crunching gently beneath her shoes, her eyes adjusting to the shadowed stretch of horizon as it unfolded before her.

And then she saw him. Ethan.

Standing just a few steps away, his back to her, facing the view from the ridge on which the house had been built. His frame cut an imposing shape against the backdrop, tall, wide, still. His hands were clasped neatly behind his back, posture straight like a man trained to listen before speaking.

He looked like a wall.

Unmoved.

Unbothered.

Unshaken.

Sophia stopped in her tracks and stared. She turned her full body toward him , something instinctive, something she didn't plan. The breeze tugged at her shirt, her hair swaying lightly, her breath still uneven from the emotions she thought she'd buried inside the house. Her throat was dry, her mind still cloudy, and her heart a little too raw.

Nobody from New York would've recognized her like this. No expensive heels. No guarded stare. No tailored poise.

Just… her. Sophia Carter. Worn. Quiet. Disarmed.

Ethan didn't move. Didn't speak. Without even turning to her, he lifted his arm slightly and held out a water bottle in her direction.

She blinked. Surprised by the gesture.

She hesitated not because she didn't need it, but because it felt strangely intimate. Unexpected. But she reached forward, took it from his hand, and brought it to her lips.

The water was cool. Calming. Her chest lifted in a quiet exhale.

There was something in the act of taking what was offered that made her feel… something she didn't quite have words for.

Submissive?

No , not exactly.

Open, maybe.

Unshielded.

Perhaps because she wasn't in her senses today. Perhaps because she was too broken, too sentimental, cracked open at the core in a way she hadn't allowed herself to be in decades. Otherwise, on any other day, she would've kept that water bottle to the ground and taught him a lesson in boundaries.

But today wasn't that day. And he wasn't just any man.

She drank again, then lowered the bottle. The silence prevailed longer between then or perhaps over the entire Willow Creek.

She turned her gaze away from the horizon and back to him, her voice low but pointed.

"How can you judge someone you just met a few minutes ago?"

His head turned slightly. The angle of his face shifted, and she could see his profile; tight jaw, drawn lips, those eyes.

Those eyes were sharp, shooting a glare into hers, or as if searching the authenticity of her question.

And… red? Yes, his eyes seemed blood-shot, she didn't know why though.

He didn't reply right away. Instead, he looked at her. Fully. Deeply.

As if searching for something buried behind her lashes. The silence between them deepened. Then he turned his gaze away.

Sophia narrowed her eyes.She wasn't finished.

She wasn't sure what she was trying to say, not exactly, but she couldn't let it drop. Her voice faltered as she tried again. "Nobody ever talked to me like that."

He inhaled. Long. Slow.

And then, she opened her mouth to speak again, voice firmer, tone rising,

"Do you have any idea, "

"Sorry." He said it so quietly. So sharply. One word. Clipped. Clean. And final. It silenced her.

She stared at him, stunned.

He didn't even let her finish her sentence. Didn't let her tell him who she was. What she had achieved. Why she didn't deserve to be spoken to like some ordinary girl standing beside a broken-down estate.

He just… apologized.

Without conditions.

Without asking for her resume.

Without even needing to know.

And that, somehow, made it worse. She clenched the water bottle tighter in her hand. She wanted to shout, Don't you want to know who I am? She wanted to say, Do you even understand what I've done? What I've built?

But he didn't wait. He turned, walked toward the horses, and without looking back, mounted the black stallion with the ease of a man who knew when to leave a moment alone. He turned just slightly in the saddle, his eyes hidden under the brim of his hat.

"Do you want to see anything else?"

She stared at him. Her lips parted. But no words came. Then she looked up at the sky, at the falling light. "No," she said finally. "It's late. I'll better go home."

She walked toward the white horse, ran her hand once over its mane, then mounted with the same practiced grace she had shown earlier. No one watching her would've guessed her heart was still thrumming in her chest like a question she couldn't answer.

The ride back was silent. Utterly and entirely silent. No words. No glances.

Just the quiet rhythm of hooves on dirt. The chirping of insects. The occasional cry of a bird finding its way home.

Sophia didn't look at Ethan.

But Ethan?

He looked at her. Quietly. Often. She didn't notice. Or maybe she did. But didn't let herself react.

To him, she looked like someone buried in memory, still seated in the room they had left behind, her soul still curled up on the floor beside her grandfather's bed. Her body moved with the horse, but her eyes were far, far away.

And he couldn't look away.

Because somehow, with the sun setting behind her, her figure draped in the amber light, her hair catching the last golden rays , she looked more beautiful than the entire dawn across Willow Creek.

She looked like someone who wasn't trying to be seen.

Which made her… unforgettable.

That night passed slowly, not in hours, but in thoughts. Sophia lay still beneath the light cotton sheets of her room, her eyes fixed on the ceiling, the fan spinning slow circles above her as if mocking her sleeplessness. No emails. No phone buzzing beside her. No meetings to wake up for.

But sleep never came.

She tossed lightly, turned once, then settled again, but nothing silenced the reverberation of the empty hallways of her childhood home and the repetition of Ethan's words from earlier.

Why are you so afraid of crying in front of someone?

The way he'd said it, not just the words, but the look in his eyes when he did. And that one word, sorry, so sharp, so final, as if he'd already understood the conversation she didn't know how to finish.

By the time morning filtered through the curtains in pale gold ribbons, her thoughts hadn't rested, and neither had she.

A gentle breeze stirred the soft cotton of her nightgown, a muted beige maxi with lace trim at the sleeves. She wrapped her hands around a warm ceramic mug of coffee, the scent of it somehow grounding her, as she stood by the window and stared out at the slow-moving life of Willow Creek.

From her window, she could see the village slowly waking. Sunlight danced lazily over tiled rooftops, smoke rose in light trails from a nearby chimney, and two children chased a wooden hoop down a dirt road, their laughter too honest for the world Sophia knew.

And then… she saw him.

Ethan.

Riding that same black horse, his figure cut sharp against the morning haze. She didn't move.

He didn't call out. Not right away. He caught sight of her , watching through her window , and the moment their eyes met, he raised one hand in a simple wave. Nothing dramatic. Just acknowledgment.

And then came that smile again. The one he wore so easily. Too easily. The kind that felt like a sunrise you didn't want to believe in. He gestured toward her with a slight tilt of his head and lifted his hand again, motioning for her to come down.

She stared back, unmoving.

Not resistant.

Just still.

Still Sophia Carter.

A woman whose silences spoke more than most people's shouting. But still, something in the air softened, maybe the wind, maybe the moment. She turned from the window, quietly, like someone answering a call she didn't want to admit she'd heard.

Moments later, she stepped outside, same night maxi, bare arms, coffee still in hand. Her hair was loosely tied back, a few strands brushing her cheek with every shift of the breeze. She wasn't dressed for morning rides or social smiles, and yet… she didn't turn around.

Ethan tugged at the reins as the horse stilled before her. He remained mounted, his eyes squinting slightly beneath the brim of his hat, the morning sun painting shadows across his face.

"Hello," he said, voice lighter again. That charming casualness had returned as though nothing heavy had passed between them. "My only customer."

She didn't respond.

He grinned wider, trying again. "Come on. Let me show you more of Willow Creek."

Sophia sipped her coffee, eyes narrowed slightly in that same unreadable way. No amusement. No rejection either. Just… listening.

"Look around," he added, gesturing at the sky with a tilt of his chin. "You ever seen weather this welcoming? If it had arms, it'd hug you."

She still said nothing.

He sighed, playful but patient. "You're a tourist here, whether you admit it or not."

She raised a brow. "I'm not here for sightseeing."

"I know," he said, his tone shifting only slightly still playful, but just enough sincerity to keep her from turning away. "Which is why I'm not offering a tour guide package. Just a ride."

Sophia hesitated. Then, in her quiet, careful way, she said, "I'm sorry for assuming you were some kind of… horse guide."

He laughed. "It's alright. You were convincing."

Her eyes lifted, meeting his gaze. "But why did you come again?" she asked, genuinely this time.

Ethan tilted his head. "To show you Willow Creek," he said softly.

"I told you," she murmured. "I don't want to see it."

His eyes searched her for a moment, not pressing.

"Why not?"

"I've seen it already."

There was a long pause. The kind that breathes.

Then he said, quieter this time, "Then maybe… to help you with whatever you came here to do."

The words struck. Not hard. Not fast. But deeply.

Sophia blinked.

He wasn't guessing now or at least she thought so, as if he knew something. Not everything. But just enough to make her throat tighten.

She turned her head slightly, staring toward the field where the wildflowers now bloomed, the ones her grandmother had once grown in neat rows.

And she nodded.

Just once.

Almost imperceptible.

Then, brushing her hand through her hair, she mumbled, "Give me ten minutes to change."

Ethan's face broke into a boyish grin, all relief and mischief.

"I'll be here," he said.

And with a light nudge, his horse gave that short, eager sound again, a soft neigh, a shuffle of hooves, before he turned it toward the road, circling once like a promise and waiting under the shade of an elm tree.

Sophia stood still a second longer and watched him. She wondered who exactly he was, not in name, but in spirit. Because that morning, when he smiled at her like nothing had broken the day before… she believed it. Even if only for a second.

Sophia had faced investors with trembling markets, hostile panels in rooms filled with men who doubted her, and deadlines that threatened to collapse the spine of her empire, but nothing had ever made her stare at a mirror quite like this.

She stood in the quiet room of the inn, barefoot on cool wooden flooring, coffee gone cold on the nightstand. A pale, full-length pink maxi clung to her frame gently, flowing like early morning light. The color, soft and undeniably girlish, looked so unlike the woman who usually wore stone hues and silver watches.

She bit her lip.

It was a color meant for someone unguarded. Someone who smiled easily. She had neither of those traits.

Her hands hovered near her hair, should she let it flow? Tie it back? Which version of herself did she want to take out into Willow Creek?

She hadn't felt this unsure in years.

After all, dressing had always been a function of purpose: commanding rooms, projecting authority, controlling how much or how little people saw. But now? Now she was dressing for... a ride. For him.

And it annoyed her that she cared.

She adjusted the hem of her dress, ran her fingers over the delicate lace at the sleeve, and sat down to buckle her sandals. A thin, silver bracelet caught her eye. She reached for it. Then paused.

She had worn it last on her sixteenth birthday. A gift from her grandfather. Back then, it had hung loose around her wrist. Now it slid perfectly over her bone. She fastened it slowly. Then stood.

Something crossed her mind and she ran to the cupboard, took out that vintage box, opened it, took out an envelope containing that cream-colored letter, put it in her bag. Took one last look. And walked out.

Outside, Ethan was already waiting. Perched atop his black horse, back straight, boots resting in the stirrups like he belonged there. He looked like a man who knew how to wait. Like he wasn't in a hurry to be anywhere else.

When he saw her, his posture changed slightly. He didn't say anything at first. Just... looked.

And Sophia felt it , the way his gaze moved from her eyes to her dress, not in a way that objectified her, but in the way someone stares when they're unexpectedly struck by something gentle.

Then came the grin.

It grew slowly, stretching across his face like it had been waiting all morning.

"Morning," he said, tipping his hat.

Sophia nodded, keeping her expression carefully neutral. "Morning."

He looked her over again, then added, "Is that what tourists wear now?"

She lifted a brow, her voice as dry as the road beneath them. "Is that what cowboys wear?"

He laughed, a quick bark of humor. "Touché."

Sophia crossed her arms. "You said something about showing me the village?"

He held out a hand, still smiling. "Come on. Hop up. Let me show you Willow Creek the way you really should see it."

She hesitated.

Then stepped forward and allowed him to help her mount. His hand on hers was warm, firm, but not invasive.

Once she was seated, they rode.

Through narrow paths framed by hedges, over tiny bridges that curved gently across creeks, past wildflowers that spilled onto the dirt road like nature had given up trying to keep tidy.

They didn't speak much at first. But the silence between them didn't ache. It settled. Like dust in sunlight.

Then Ethan glanced sideways and said, "You wear pink well."

Sophia turned to him, caught off guard. "Not something I wear often."

"I figured."

She waited, letting the pause hang.

"I just didn't think you ever would," he added.

"And why's that?"

"You don't strike me as someone who chooses softness."

She tilted her head. "Maybe I wore it today to remind myself that softness still exists."

He looked at her a long moment, his eyes steady, but no longer teasing. "Then I'm glad I got to see it."

She looked away.

Because if she didn't, she might've smiled and she wasn't ready to give him that.

Ethan cleared his throat. "So, where are we in the grand mystery?"

Sophia raised an eyebrow. "What mystery?"

"Come on," he said, nudging his horse slightly closer. "You came all this way. Alone. You've spent the last few days running from ghosts in a house that remembers you more than you let on."

"I didn't come to chase ghosts," she said, firm.

CHAPTER 8: THE STORM BEFORE PEACE

The first drop was so subtle it could've been the breath of a leaf. Sophia flinched anyway.

It brushed her cheek like a cold secret, feather-light and gone too soon. She paused, looked up , and there it was. The sky had changed its mind. What was once soft and gentle had now turned into a threatening gray, its heavy clouds gathering like an audience before a storm.

A chill slipped through the air.

Then came the wind, not strong, but pointed, like the prelude to something important.

And before she could fully register the shift, the heavens cracked open.

Rain poured down.

Not a drizzle.

Not a polite shower. A full-throated, unapologetic downpour.

The dry dirt path beneath the hooves of their horses darkened instantly, soaking into the earth like ink spilled across parchment. Water collected in grooves and puddles.

The air was alive now, humming with the rhythm of rain , the sound relentless, wild, intimate.

Sophia was horrified.

"What the, Oh my God!" she gasped, ducking instinctively and trying to shield herself with her hands. "No, no, no… This is insane!"

She fumbled at her shoulders, tugging helplessly at the wet fabric of her dress, which clung to her like a second skin. Her long pale pink maxi, once a canva of softness and simplicity, now turned translucent , painting every curve, every flaw she tried so hard to hide.

Her sandals squelched against the stirrups. Her curls, so carefully tucked, were now sticking to her forehead, neck, and jawline in messy tendrils. The rain spared no one, least of all someone as polished, as distant, as controlled as Sophia Carter.

"This is a nightmare," she muttered, nearly out of breath, teeth chattering lightly. "I've never bathed in rain before, and I'm not starting now!"

She turned, ready to unleash all her frustration, only to find Ethan… completely unaffected.

Of course.

He was sitting still on his horse, relaxed, looking up at the sky like it was a friend who had just shown up without knocking.

His dark shirt had turned nearly black, soaked and clinging to his chest and arms, the fabric molded to muscle and broad bone. His hat, useless now, was pushed back slightly, and water trickled from his temple down into the stubble lining his jaw.

But he didn't seem bothered. Not even a little. He was calm. Wild. As if he belonged to this storm.

The contrast between them was so clear and.

"If you'd stop complaining for just a second," he said, voice raised only enough to beat the sound of the rain, "you might actually enjoy it."

Sophia blinked.

"Enjoy it?" she shouted back. "Are you insane? Do you even know how expensive this dress is? My shoes are ruined! My hair is, "

Ethan tilted his head slightly, his smirk obvious even in the rain. "You done?"

She glared at him. "No!"

He exhaled, clearly amused, and looked up toward the sky again.

"Let it," he said softly.

"Let what?" she snapped, wiping her face furiously.

"Let it soak you."

Sophia stared.

"This isn't a novel, Ethan! This is real life!"

But he didn't argue. Didn't push. Just looked at her, then let his eyes drift away again.

And suddenly… it clicked. Something about the way he sat. The way he breathed. He wasn't challenging her. He was offering her something she didn't know she needed. A moment to stop resisting. A moment to exist.

For a long beat, Sophia hesitated. Her fingers still clutched her reins like they were handles to her pride. But then, like a murmur in the back of her mind, something changed.

She loosened her grip. And tilted her head back. The rain hit her face, and for the first time in years, she didn't flinch.

She felt it.

The freedom of it. The absurdity. The purity. And in that suspended moment between one inhale and the next, she let go.

She laughed. Soft at first. Then louder, breathless and unrecognizable. She threw her arms out slightly, letting the water claim her. Her heart beat faster, not with panic, but with presence.

Sophia Carter, the woman who never let herself fall, was finally letting go. Ethan turned slowly, watching her in stunned silence. And when she caught his eye, she smiled, not carefully, not with caution.

A real, rain-soaked smile.

"Better?" he asked.

She nodded, still catching her breath. "Much."

They rode on , slower now, with no rush, the road a ribbon of silver beneath their horses.

"You ever going to admit that was your first time?" he asked, smirking.

"In the rain?" she replied. "Yes."

"And?"

She looked over her shoulder. "I still think it's ridiculous."

He chuckled. "But freeing."

She turned back to the view ahead. "Yes."

And so, they spend hours flying in the sky over their horse, playing and dancing in the rain as droplets of water until the night wore on and darkness spread all around. Then, he took her back to the hotel but instead of leaving here there, to her surprise, he also entered in to the restaurant chamber.

The warmth of the café pressed around Sophia like a blanket freshly pulled from the dryer. The crackling from the hearth mixed with soft laughter from across the room, and even the gleaming candlelight on each table seemed to lean in closer, gently whispering: stay a little longer.

She stirred her soup slowly, letting the spoon sink and rise again. Every sip melted something inside her that had been cold for years , not just from the rain, but from the weight of carrying so much alone.

Across from her, Ethan sat casually, elbows on the table, hands wrapped around his mug. He hadn't said much since they came in, but he didn't have to. His presence was enough.

Around them, the hum of conversation swirled gently, and Sophia found herself listening in between bites. Names she didn't know, places she half-remembered, stories she wasn't a part of but strangely wanted to be. She had no idea how long they sat like that , two outsiders in different ways, one of them just beginning to admit it.

Then her gaze drifted across the café wall.

Photographs, dozens of them, lined the wooden planks like a mosaic of lives long entwined. Kids running through meadows, families at harvest festivals, elders smiling under porch lights. Most were in color, some old enough to have faded into sepia.

But one… stopped her breath.

Near the far-left side, crooked slightly in its frame, was a photograph that didn't match the rest.

Black and white.

Crisp.

A little girl in a white frock, standing between an older man and woman, in front of a ridge-top house that hadn't changed in structure but looked freshly painted in the photo.

Her lips parted slightly.

She didn't move and her eyes locked onto the image.

That… that was her.

She knew the way her hand curled into her grandmother's dress.

She knew the watch on her grandfather's wrist.

She knew that this photo was taken the day before everything changed.

Without a word, she stood.

Ethan followed her gaze and slowly turned. She walked to the wall, her fingers reaching toward the glass but hovering just short of touching.

"Aunt Maggie?" she asked, her voice quieter than usual.

The older woman looked up from across the room and smiled. "Yes, sweetheart?"

Sophia nodded toward the photo. "Where did you get this?"

Maggie crossed the café slowly, wiping her hands on her apron. "That? Oh, that's one of the oldest ones here. That was taken by my brother. He used to run around the Ridge with a camera like it was a rifle. Said he was capturing memories so the town wouldn't forget them."

Sophia blinked. "He knew them?"

Maggie looked at her carefully, then nodded.

"Everyone knew the Carters," she said softly. "Mr. Carter… he wasn't just respected. He was loved. And Mrs Carter, she made the best lemon tarts anyone ever tasted."

Sophia felt her throat tighten.

Ethan stepped beside Sophia; his expression unreadable.

Sophia didn't look at him. She kept her eyes on the photo. But her heart… Her heart was loud now.

Because suddenly, Willow Creek didn't feel like the past. It felt like a door that had been waiting patiently to be opened again.

Sophia had spent years surrounded by people in boardrooms with a dozen eager executives, on stages beneath bright lights, behind glass doors where her name conveyed respect but still she had never felt more isolated than in those moments when she was applauded most.

But now, in this quiet, fire-warmed café tucked away in a village she'd nearly erased from memory, something stirred inside her. Something she didn't yet have a name for.

She sat wrapped in a towel that smelled faintly of lavender and woodsmoke, the fabric soft around her shoulders. Her long pink maxi, now soaked and slightly clinging to her legs, felt like the least remarkable thing about her , which was strange. She had spent so much of her life carefully assembling her image. And yet now, with rain-tangled curls hanging loose around her face and no eyeliner left on her lashes, she felt… real.

The room itself seemed to vibrate with an old, familiar magic. It didn't murmur welcome, it simply assumed you belonged. The walls were wooden and timeworn had heard hundreds of stories. Each table bore signs of wear, small nicks, uneven edges but no one noticed. The shelves sagged under books that had clearly been read and re-read, their spines cracked, dog-eared corners proud of their journeys. Framed photos, most in black and white or sun-faded color, told their own silent stories. Little ceramic figurines and painted plates lined the windowsills like sentries of memory.

The people inside weren't strangers. They were each other's furniture. Their conversations overlapped like layers of a song, laughter rising here and there without the self-consciousness of big-city cafés. No one glanced her way with that peculiar curiosity she was used to that measured, evaluated, recognized.

Here, no one asked who she was. And for some reason, that made her chest tighten.

Across from her, Ethan sat with an effortless grace she both admired and resented. His navy shirt, damp and clinging in places, didn't seem to bother him. He leaned back in his chair, sipping coffee, watching the room like a man who had memorized its every detail long ago.

He belonged here. In a way that felt almost mythical.

He didn't dominate the space; he dissolved into it. People nodded to him in passing with subtle familiarity, but they didn't hover. They didn't interrupt. It was the kind of respect that came without demand, earned not by power, but by presence.

Sophia stirred the bowl of soup in front of her. It was hearty, thick with root vegetables and fresh herbs, and smelled like something that had been simmering for hours.

She took a careful sip. And stopped. It wasn't just good. It was comforting in a way she hadn't experienced. It bypassed her taste buds and went straight to her chest, warming something that had been cold far too long.

She took another spoonful. Slower this time.

Around her, the world remained easy, alive. A child read aloud from a picture book near the hearth. A man in a wool cap leaned close to his wife to whisper something that made her laugh. A young couple fed each other spoonfuls of dessert without looking embarrassed.

Sophia had spent a lifetime in restaurants where the price of the wine mattered more than the person across the table. She'd built a life on achievement, forward motion, strategy.

But these people?

They weren't trying to build anything.

They were living.

And that realization unsettled her too in a way that made her grip the soup bowl a little tighter. A hand, gentle, warm touched her shoulder.

She turned, startled. An older woman with kind eyes and salt-and-pepper hair offered her a motherly smile.

"You poor thing," she said softly, the corners of her eyes crinkling. "Make sure you finish it, love. Nothing gets rid of a storm chill like this soup."

Sophia blinked.

"…Thank you," she said, the words unfamiliar on her tongue.

The woman smiled again and moved on. Sophia turned back to the table, her thoughts spinning. No one had fussed over her like that in years. Not since...

She didn't let the thought finish.

Ethan hadn't said a word during the exchange. But when she looked at him, he was watching her , not studying, not analyzing. Just… watching.

And she didn't flinch from it. She didn't feel exposed. Just… seen.

The silence between them stretched , but not uncomfortably. It wasn't the silence of things unsaid. It was the silence of being allowed to exist without performance.

"I've never eaten soup like this," she murmured, her voice low.

Ethan gave a small smirk. "You've probably never eaten soup made in a kitchen with no timer, no recipe, and no pressure."

She looked down at the bowl. "It tastes like something my grandmother would've made."

He said nothing. But she felt the shift in the air, the silence that respects the burden of a memory.

"I don't remember much about her," Sophia added. "But I remember warmth like this."

Ethan reached for his mug and took a slow sip. "Sometimes memory hides in taste more than thought."

They didn't speak for a long while.

The warmth from the fire, the food, the people, it wrapped around her until she couldn't tell if the mist on the windows was from the rain outside or the quiet melting happening within her.

She felt… light. And that terrified her. Because she didn't know how to carry lightness anymore. But tonight, she didn't have to carry anything. Tonight, she just had to finish her soup. And maybe if the world allowed, to let herself believe she was safe enough to stay seated at the table.

The warmth of the café had settled deep into Sophia's bones not just against the dampness of her clothes or the sting of wind-kissed skin, but somewhere far deeper. Somewhere hollow. Somewhere lonely.

And she hadn't realized it was lonely until now.

The storm outside had stilled. The occasional droplet slid down the windows in lazy streaks, the clouds outside drifting like tired ships over the rooftops of Willow Creek. Inside, it was soft. Dim. Golden. The type of golden that reminded her of honey warmed over a stove, rich, calming, and slow.

Her soup bowl sat nearly empty before her, and the space around her had shifted, not with noise, but with ease. It had been so long since she sat in a place that didn't demand anything from her.

And yet, here, in this village café filled with strangers, she didn't feel like she was being measured.

Across the room, a woman , apron creased and powdered with flour , approached their table, carrying a plate of biscuits glazed in honey. She set it down in front of Sophia with a soft smile, her voice quiet but warm.

"These help after the rain," she said. "Especially if the storm got through more than just your coat."

Sophia looked at the biscuits. She didn't know what to say at first. But she nodded. "Thank you."

"Take two," the woman added with a small chuckle, already walking away. "We don't let anyone leave chilled."

Sophia reached for one, the edges still warm to the touch, sticky with syrup. She brought it to her lips, took a bite. And stopped. It was soft. But not delicate. Sweet, but not loud. It reminded her of something she couldn't name.

As she chewed slowly, the atmosphere around her softened. Not because anything had changed , but because she had.

She glanced up. The villagers were talking about the rain , its timing, the freshness it left in the fields, the way it had knocked the last apples from the trees. Some speculated whether it would flood the lower bridge again. Others spoke of their gardens, of boots soaked through, of dogs refusing to go outside.

Simple things. Real things.

No one asked what she did for a living. No one glanced at her shoes. No one tried to assess her worth in numbers or titles or influence. They simply were.

And somehow… it left her breathless. Without realizing, she shifted ever so slightly, closer to Ethan.

Just a few inches. But he noticed. Of course, he noticed.

Still, he didn't say anything. He didn't tease. Didn't raise a brow. He let her have the space she needed to breathe.

She sat like that for a while, watching the room, listening to the soft murmur of conversation, feeling the honey dissolve on her tongue. And then she whispered it, not to him, not to anyone really, but to herself.

"They're happy."

Ethan glanced at her, quiet. "Who?"

"These people," she replied, looking around. "All of them. They're happy."

He followed her gaze. Then nodded once. "Yeah. They are."

Sophia frowned. "Why?"

He didn't blink. "Because they have enough."

"Enough?" she repeated.

"Enough to live," he said, his voice lower now. "Enough to rest. Enough to care about small things. Enough to not want more."

She looked down at her biscuit. It was almost gone.

"Enough," she repeated, quieter this time. She couldn't even remember the last time she felt she had enough , not of money, not of work, but of… stillness.

And in a strange twist of thought, she realized something bitter. She'd had too much. Too much pressure. Too much isolation. Too much distance between who she was and what the world expected her to be.

Her throat tightened.

But she didn't speak.

She just sat , with it.

The café's golden lights gleamed slightly as the wind kissed the windows again, soft and brief. The fire crackled near the far wall. Someone began tuning a guitar in the corner. The kind of life Sophia had only ever seen in books was happening in front of her, around her, without needing her to participate.

It just was. And she was welcome to watch it.

The bowl in front of her was nearly empty. The plate of biscuits sat with only one remaining.

She exhaled.

And once in days , maybe weeks , she wasn't thinking about the inbox in her phone. She wasn't thinking about strategies, schedules, or silence. She was simply... breathing.

Then Ethan's voice broke through, soft but steady. "Should we go?"

She blinked, pulled back from her thoughts.

"Where?" she asked, almost sleepily.

"You mentioned the library," he said evenly. "You said you needed internet. To check in."

The words hit her like cold water.

The library.

The emails.

Her company.

New York.

She sat upright. Her heart stuttered. How had she forgotten? How could she have sat here, in this place of peace, while a dozen crises might be burning behind the scenes of her life? She pushed back from the table, too fast. The chair scraped against the floor, loud and awkward. A few heads turned. She didn't notice. All she felt was panic rising in her throat like a threat.

She looked at Ethan, her voice catching. "I forgot, I need to, "

But then she stopped. Because the look in his eyes had changed.

He hadn't moved. But something in his face , in the way his jaw tightened slightly, the way his gaze held hers without expression , told her everything. He wasn't angry. But the softness from earlier? It was gone.

And that stung. He stood slowly, without a word.

His movements weren't rushed, weren't cold , but they had burden. As if something he'd been holding onto had quietly slipped from his hands.

Sophia's chest ached. But she didn't know what to say. And he didn't wait for her to find it. Together, they stepped out into the night air.

But the warmth between them? That had stayed behind.

CHAPTER 9: THE SILENT SAVIOUR

Ethan led Sophia quietly into Willow Creek's modest public library, a cozy refuge nestled between quaint houses and weathered stone paths, the village's heart wrapped in silence after the storm. Sophia had barely dried from the rain; her pink dress clung gently to her skin, her hair now loose and slightly damp. She stepped hesitantly onto the worn wooden floors, the gentle scent of polished wood and old paper curling softly in the air.

The silence and warmth inside contrasted sharply with the tension simmering between them. She followed Ethan to the librarian's desk, watching as he approached with a quiet confidence that felt almost foreign to her. She couldn't quite hear their exchange, only murmured words, a faint rustle as Ethan handed over some cash, and a gentle nod of understanding from the elderly librarian.

Sophia was taken aback, more by Ethan's casual authority than the action itself. He hadn't asked if she needed assistance or checked if she had money. He had simply handled the situation with calm assurance. A flutter of unease stirred in her chest; she had always managed every detail of her life, every step meticulously planned, never allowing anyone close enough to do something like this for her.

Ethan turned toward her, his voice flat, betraying no emotion. "You're all set. You can use the internet without needing a card."

She hesitated, swallowing down the sudden knot in her throat. There was a subtle shift in his tone, resigned, distant, as if he'd quietly closed a door between them. She opened her mouth slightly, ready to question it, but the pull of the outside world, her world, was stronger. She couldn't loiter on this uncertain ache right now.

Nodding briefly, she turned away and hurried toward a small wooden table bathed in the warm, amber glow of a reading lamp. Her fingers moved automatically, slipping out her laptop, connecting swiftly to the Wi-Fi, and instantly, her familiar world came flooding back. Notifications flashed, emails loaded swiftly, each red badge blinking urgently as though the world had held its breath for her return.

Without hesitating, she dialed the familiar number, her heartbeat quickening as the phone rang once before her assistant's anxious voice flooded the line.

"Miss Sophia!" the assistant exclaimed breathlessly, relief and concern mingling. "We were starting to panic,"

"Status update," Sophia interrupted smoothly, her tone even and unshakable, as if the warmth of the café and the softness of the rain had never touched her at all.

Her assistant paused for only a heartbeat before diving into professional mode. "Right, yes. The investor meeting was rescheduled, the German deal was finalized without issues, marketing managed the campaign delay, and there's nothing major outstanding."

Sophia listened intently, her posture perfectly straight, her eyes locked onto the glowing screen as if reconnecting to her former self. The relaxed woman who had laughed in the rain, who had eaten honey-drizzled biscuits with uncertain delight, was quickly fading, replaced by a figure carved from quiet power and control.

Across the library, Ethan sat near a tall, rain-speckled window, his gaze fixed not on the fading storm outside but inwardly, toward her. He listened carefully to the sharpness of her voice, the clipped, decisive manner in which she reclaimed authority, and something in his expression softened briefly into an understated smile, not mocking, nor amused, but one born of quiet admiration.

Beneath that faint pride simmered a bittersweet ache. Because while he admired her strength, he mourned the loss of the woman who had hesitantly leaned closer to him at the café, who had allowed herself to relax into an unfamiliar sense of belonging. The woman who had briefly glimpsed a different kind of life had already disappeared, swiftly replaced by the powerful figure who commanded her world from afar.

Sophia hung up the phone gently, exhaling as she ran her hand through her damp hair. Everything was stable, running perfectly without her immediate presence. The realization unsettled her more deeply than any crisis could have. She had spent her life believing her world would collapse without her constant vigilance, but it hadn't. It was strong, steady, functioning independently, and that fact left a strange ache in her chest.

Her gaze drifted to Ethan, who remained unusually silent by the window. He sat with quiet dignity, his face turned slightly away, shoulders relaxed yet somehow guarded. The warm, playful Ethan who had laughed with her earlier had retreated behind a subtle mask.

She frowned softly, frustration building as she observed the shift in him. She had glimpsed a different side of Ethan Walker earlier, someone warm and deeply embedded in the fabric of Willow Creek. Someone who's easy smiles and quiet patience had briefly touched something vulnerable within her.

Taking a quiet breath, she finally spoke, her voice soft but carrying clearly through the silent space. "I saw different sides of you today," she murmured carefully.

Ethan turned slowly from the window, his gaze meeting hers with a gentle neutrality. After a pause, a faint, humorless smirk appeared on his lips. "Oh, did you?" he replied, his voice edged lightly with irony. "Which side did you prefer, the one who arranged internet access, or the one who introduced you to small-town biscuits?"

Sophia froze, momentarily at a loss. His sharp comment caught her off-guard, the casual dismissal of what she'd thought was a meaningful admission leaving her uncertain. She'd been close to something deeper, standing at the edge of vulnerability, and with a single comment, he had neatly sidestepped it.

She felt oddly betrayed, though she knew she had no right to feel that way. Her lips parted, words hovering uncertainly before retreating. Ethan's small smirk remained, but it had softened into something weary and resigned.

He stood up slowly, stretching with a casual air that somehow felt distant, detached. His gaze briefly flicked back toward her, guarded yet quietly intense. "Well," he said softly, a faint smile playing at his lips, "I guess your world is calling you back now. No reason to loiter here, is there?"

Sophia felt herself tense slightly, her fingers brushing restlessly over the wooden table as she struggled to respond. "I …" she started, then faltered, uncertain. She wanted to deny his words, to explain the inexplicable pull she felt toward this tiny village and its quiet streets, to the honeyed air of the café, and even to him. But no suitable words appeared.

Ethan's quiet gaze softened briefly, almost as if hoping she'd say something more. But when she didn't, he merely offered a slight shrug. "I'll walk your back," he murmured, his voice gentle yet tinged with finality.

Without waiting, he moved toward the door, opening it and holding it quietly, his eyes fixed ahead, no longer searching for hers.

She rose slowly, collecting her belongings in silence. The walk back was quiet, the distance between them now tangible, a soft, sad ache settling between every careful step.

The easy closeness from earlier had vanished, replaced by cautious distance. Sophia felt a gentle sadness she couldn't quite name. She had briefly glimpsed another life, another possibility. But now, walking quietly beside Ethan under the misty evening sky, she sensed clearly the gulf between their worlds.

And she realized, with a silent pang of regret, that Ethan knew it too.

The rain had softened the village into a watercolor painting, the world glistening gently beneath the dim glow of streetlamps. The storm's departure had left behind a peaceful lull, the silence cut only by the faint dripping of water from eaves and branches, and the distant murmur of a creek swollen by rainwater. Sophia walked beside Ethan, their footsteps crunching softly against gravel paths, the space between them comfortable, yet weighted with the unspoken.

She paused suddenly in the middle of the path, tilting her face up toward the misty, star-scattered sky. Ethan halted beside her, eyebrows raised slightly in curiosity.

"What is it?" he asked, voice gentle, cautious.

She hesitated, biting her lip as though embarrassed by her own thought. "I don't want to go back indoors yet," she admitted softly, her voice so quiet that he almost missed it. "It feels... good out here. Can we walk a little longer?"

Ethan smiled slowly, a burst of warmth spreading through his chest. *I was hoping you'd say that,* he said to himself without words then he replied softly. "Walking in the village after rain is one of the best parts about living here."

She glanced at him, her lips twitching into a cautious, genuine smile. "You do this often?"

"More than I'd admit publicly," he said, the edges of his eyes crinkling warmly. "People might think I'm losing it, wandering around at night."

Sophia chuckled lightly, relaxing visibly. "Maybe you are."

"Possibly," he shrugged lightly, feigning seriousness. "But you seem just as likely a candidate, wandering around here with me."

She rolled her eyes softly, but the corners of her mouth lifted further. "Maybe insanity is contagious in Willow Creek," she suggested playfully.

"Maybe," he conceded, his eyes holding hers gently. "Or maybe you're finally catching onto why the locals seem happier than most people you've ever met."

Sophia considered that for a moment, letting the silence loiter comfortably between them. "Maybe you're right," she admitted, voice barely above a whisper.

They started walking again, their steps slow and deliberate, as if trying to stretch every second beneath the open sky. The village felt surreal, quaint cottages shimmering under the wet glow, small gardens smelling of lavender and rain-soaked earth, the air cool and rich with renewal.

"I think what surprises me most," she spoke finally, softly contemplative, "is how open everyone is here. It's like... they've known each other their entire lives. There's no pretense, no hidden agendas."

Ethan nodded slowly. "Small town life. Everyone knows everything about each other. That can be both a comfort and a curse."

She tilted her head thoughtfully, considering his words. "But don't you ever feel... suffocated? Or limited?"

He glanced sideways at her, smiling faintly. "I used to," he admitted. "When I was younger, all I wanted was to leave Willow Creek and see everything the world had to offer."

"What changed?"

He exhaled quietly; eyes distant but warm. "I left. I traveled a bit, saw some amazing places. But every time I woke up in a new city, I realized that I didn't feel half as free there as I felt walking these streets, talking with people I've known my whole life. It was ironic; freedom was exactly where I thought I'd left it behind."

She watched him closely, captivated by the quiet honesty in his voice. "I envy you that," she said softly. "The comfort of knowing exactly where you belong."

He looked at her curiously, head tilted slightly. "You don't feel you belong in your world?"

She hesitated, drawing in a slow breath, as though deciding how much to reveal. "I belong there in some ways," she said slowly. "In the sense that I've built something of value, something that means a great deal to many people. But in terms of... peace?" She shook her head gently. "No. I've never belonged that way."

Her response left him speechless for a long while as if he had not expected that, or instead, he had expected the quite opposite.

"Why not?" he pressed softly, sensing her willingness to speak more openly now. "You're obviously incredibly capable, and clearly respected, as far as I have noted when you were on the phone call with your company mates."

She looked down, carefully avoiding his gaze, her voice suddenly fragile. "Because I've always felt like an outsider, even in my own life," she admitted. "Every move I've made, every decision, every triumph, it feels like I've been watching someone else achieve them. Like my life was meant for somebody else."

He nodded gently, understanding deeply. "Maybe you've just never stopped long enough to recognize yourself in your own reflection."

She smiled faintly, sadness coloring her eyes. "Maybe," she whispered. "Until today, I don't think I've ever slowed down enough to even see what I'm missing."

They kept walking silently, the rhythm of their footsteps matching the slow beating of their hearts. Sophia glanced at him, a teasing glint returning to her eyes. "What about you, Ethan? Don't you ever get bored here?"

"Me? Bored?" He shook his head, grinning playfully. "Impossible. Willow Creek provides endless entertainment. Just yesterday, I watched Mrs. Anderson argue passionately with her roses about growing faster."

Sophia laughed, surprised and delighted. "She argued with her roses?"

"Absolutely. And believe me, the roses listened." He winked. "They always bloom perfectly for her every year."

She chuckled, feeling lighter than she had in years. "Well, who knew roses were so obedient?"

"Everyone in Willow Creek," he said solemnly. "You'll catch on soon enough."

"Maybe," she mused gently, eyes glittering with playful defiance. "Though it might take more than obedient roses to convince me."

He smirked softly, the corners of his eyes crinkling again. "Challenge accepted."

She laughed softly, shaking her head. "I've never met someone who makes absurdity sound so charming."

"It's one of my best skills," he said proudly. "Right up there with making excellent coffee and terrible pancakes."

She arched an eyebrow curiously. "Terrible pancakes?"

He nodded, mock-seriously. "Absolutely. They're legendary around here for being burnt, misshapen, but oddly delicious. People think it's deliberate."

"And is it?"

"Definitely not. But I'll never tell them that."

She laughed openly now, the sound ringing softly between the village houses. Ethan's expression warmed deeply at the genuine joy in her face, and he felt a quiet ache of affection tug at his heart.

Slowly, the laughter faded, leaving a gentle silence between them, tinged with comfortable intimacy. They turned down a narrow lane, trees overhead whispering softly with the breeze.

"I never expected to feel this," she murmured after a quiet moment, her voice almost a sigh. "When I came here, it was supposed to be simple. A quick visit, a glimpse into something long past. But I never imagined actually feeling something so..." She paused, searching for words. "Real."

He turned to face her gently, his voice low and earnest. "That's exactly what this place does. It sneaks past your defenses and reminds you what real life is."

She met his gaze, eyes wide with hesitant vulnerability. "I thought I'd never come back here, Ethan. It wasn't supposed to be part of my story anymore. But suddenly, I couldn't resist returning. And now, ..." She broke off, her gaze shifting away, uncertain.

"Now?" he prompted softly, encouragingly.

She drew in a breath, slowly gathering her courage. "Now it turns out the reason wasn't even The Ridge. Not really."

He frowned gently, curiosity and concern mingling in his eyes. "Then what was it?"

Sophia's voice was quiet, yet steady, unaware of the way Ethan's expression began to shift dramatically in the shadows.

"The letters," she confessed softly, almost absently, as if finally admitting it to herself. "I've been receiving letters for almost an year or perhaps more. They all are anonymous, comforting, hauntingly familiar letters. They drew me back here more than any memory ever could."

She didn't see Ethan freeze, didn't notice the shock that swiftly replaced his calm demeanor, didn't catch the stunned disbelief and hidden recognition flooding his eyes.

For Ethan Walker, it was as if the ground had suddenly vanished beneath his feet, leaving him in stunned silence, facing a revelation he had never, even in his most secret thoughts, expected.

the silence between them thickened into something palpable, as though the soft whispers of the night had paused, breathless, waiting for Sophia to continue. Her voice was fragile now, conveyed on a trembling edge, the words tumbling out without the carefully built restraint she'd worn her entire life.

"You see, Ethan," she said softly, her eyes looking beyond him, into memories she'd buried deep, "letters have always meant tragedy for me. Every time they came, it meant someone had left me behind forever. Each envelope conveyed loss, grief, and abandonment, messages from people who could no longer speak to me directly. My father, my grandmother, my grandfather, even my own mother, letters announcing their absence, their departure, their permanent silence. Everytime a letter came, it came to announce death of any of my dearest people."

She paused, her breath hitching, shoulders slightly shaking. Ethan stood motionless beside her, his heart aching quietly, unsure of what to say, afraid that even the softest interruption would silence the fragile truth now pouring from her.

"I stopped opening letters," she whispered, voice breaking gently. "I couldn't handle another goodbye. For years, I lived under the shadow of knowing that if a letter arrived, it meant someone else was gone. But then, something changed. A year ago, another letter arrived. And this time, it didn't announce death or loss. It was filled with kindness. Someone telling me that they admired me. That they missed me. That they, " She broke off, her voice wavering as tears pooled quietly in her eyes, shimmering softly beneath the streetlamps. "That they were waiting for me. Waiting for me, Ethan. Sophia Carter. Can you imagine that?"

She turned fully toward him then, her expression raw, eyes wide and glistening, tears slipping freely down her cheeks. "Someone waited for me, when my own family couldn't stay. When the very people who were supposed to love me, supposed to hold onto me, they all left. One by one, they disappeared, leaving me standing alone in the world."

Ethan stood rooted, his chest tightening with the mass of her words, his heart silently fracturing alongside hers. He could hardly breathe as she stepped closer, her eyes searching his, pleading silently for him to understand, to see her, not as the poised, powerful woman she always presented, but as the vulnerable girl who had been abandoned too many times to count.

She drew a shaky breath, her voice rising, trembling with suppressed emotion now flooding out. "I spent years, Ethan, years trying to forget, years running away from these memories, these losses. I built walls so high, I thought no one would ever get through them. I convinced myself I didn't need anyone, that no one could ever hurt me again if I didn't let them close enough."

Her voice caught sharply, a fragile sob breaking free. "But every night, the pain still found me. I've had sleep paralysis for years, night after night, waking trapped, unable to move or scream. Feeling hands that aren't there, seeing shadows that shouldn't exist. I see my mother standing by my bed, looking down at me, her eyes so sad, so disappointed, as if she still blames me for something I never understood."

Sophia took another shaking breath, hands clenched into fists as though trying desperately to hold herself together. "I've seen therapists, Ethan, more than I can count. I've talked and talked, but I never spoke the real truth. Not to them, not to anyone. I pretended I was fine, smiling for photos, for magazines, for investors. On my graduation day, " She stopped, her voice faltering again, tears falling freely down her cheeks. "I stood there, holding my diploma, smiling for the cameras, knowing I had just lost my mother. Knowing that she, the last promise I'd ever had in life, had finally broken hers."

Her eyes closed, eyelashes trembling as tears slid silently down her face. "She promised she'd come back for me. I remember standing there at the airport, just a child, begging her to stay. She smiled, kissed my forehead, and promised she'd return. But she never did. Instead, I got another letter."

She drew a ragged breath, her voice broken, barely a whisper. "My grandfather couldn't even say goodbye. He couldn't look at me when I was taken away, because he knew if he had, he'd never let me go. He died not long after, leaving another empty space inside me. And my grandmother, she used to tell me I reminded her of my father. She'd smile, touch my hair, and say that I conveyed him in my eyes, my laugh. But every time she looked at me, I knew she saw him too clearly, and it hurt her. I was never just Sophia. I was always someone else's ghost, someone else's grief."

Sophia stepped forward, closer now, her eyes desperate as they searched Ethan's face. "Do you understand how painful it is, to never be seen for who you really are? To live your life as someone else's memory, someone else's regret?"

Ethan moved forward instinctively; his heart overwhelmed by the raw vulnerability pouring from her. His hands rose gently, tenderly cupping her shoulders as if trying to steady her, trying to anchor her to this moment, to him.

"I never wanted to come back here," she whispered, her voice fragile, breaking into quiet sobs. "Willow Creek meant loss, abandonment. It meant the family who couldn't keep me. But then these letters started arriving again, someone writing with kindness, with warmth, saying they remembered me, that they admired me, that they waited for me."

She met his gaze, her eyes pleading silently for answers she knew he couldn't give. "Why would someone wait for me, Ethan? Who am I that anyone should wait for Sophia Carter? My entire life, no one stayed. Everyone I loved left. And suddenly, someone waited?"

Her voice broke completely then, tears cascading freely down her face as sobs shook her frame. She bowed her head, finally surrendering to the overwhelming grief she'd hidden for years.

Ethan's heart shattered quietly as he watched her cry openly, the strength she'd carefully crafted dissolving before him. Tenderly, he pulled her closer, wrapping his arms around her, holding her gently but securely against his chest.

He whispered softly into her hair, his voice warm, reassuring, achingly gentle. "Sophia, people left, not because of you, not because you weren't worth staying for. Life took them away, not you. You deserve to be waited for, to be admired, to be loved. You always have."

She shook her head against his chest, her voice muffled, anguished. "But how can you say that? How could you possibly know?"

He paused, his voice trembling slightly with hesitation, with the weight of something he hadn't yet admitted even to himself. "Because maybe, just maybe, I'm someone who understands what it feels like to wait for someone. Maybe I know what it is to watch and admire from afar, never sure if the person you're waiting for even knows you're alive."

She pulled back gently, eyes wide and startled, shimmering with unshed tears, looking into his face as if seeing him clearly for the very first time. "Ethan, ?"

He gazed at her softly, the gentleness in his expression almost heartbreaking. "Sophia, whoever wrote those letters, whoever waited for you, they saw the real you. The person beyond your family's shadows, beyond your grief. They saw the strength you hold so calmly, the beauty in your survival. You are worthy of being waited for."

She stared at him, her heart beating fiercely against her ribs, her breath coming shakily, feeling the words sink into her soul, patching small pieces of her brokenness back together. She leaned toward him slowly, hesitantly, until their foreheads gently touched, their breathing quietly aligning in the soft pattern of newly discovered intimacy.

The quiet moment stretched into something deep, something healing, something powerful, two souls recognizing a hidden truth, a shared longing that neither fully understood.

CHAPTER 10: THE HIDDEN LOVE

Sophia's tears fell silently at first, but soon they gave way to painful, breathless sobs, shaking her body with the force of long-buried grief. Her long-built dignity was shattered, replaced now by raw, trembling vulnerability.

Her sobs intensified, broken occasionally by hiccups that made her draw sharp, jagged breaths. Ethan watched helplessly, his heart aching for her, wishing he could absorb even a fraction of her pain. Quietly, he slipped off his jacket and wrapped it gently around her shoulders, offering her whatever comfort he could.

"Hey," he murmured softly, his voice filled with an aching tenderness. He reached into his pocket and retrieved a small water bottle he'd kept from the café earlier, gently opening it and pressing it lightly into her shaking hands. "Here, drink slowly."

Sophia took the bottle, her fingers trembling so much she nearly dropped it. She sipped carefully, the cold water soothing the burn in her throat but doing little to ease the ache in her chest. Her sobs began to subside slightly, replaced now with quiet sniffles, her breathing slowly steadying.

"I'm sorry," she whispered hoarsely, her voice barely audible as she wiped tears hastily from her reddened cheeks. "I, I didn't mean to fall apart like this."

Ethan shook his head gently, stepping closer, ensuring she could feel his quiet presence beside her. "Don't apologize. You don't have to pretend with me, Sophia."

She lifted her eyes hesitant to meet his. The softness she found there nearly broke her again. She exhaled shakily, fingers twisting anxiously around the half-empty bottle. "Everyone thinks I have everything," she started again, her voice trembling. "They think I'm the richest girl, the luckiest person alive. And you know what, Ethan?" She drew a shaky breath, eyes glistening with unshed tears. "I'm the poorest girl in the world. I have money, I have status, and people respect me, but nobody loves me. Not really. My house is so big, so grand, but do you know what it sounds like inside?"

He watched her silently, waiting for her to speak, giving her space to finally release all she'd conveyed silently for years.

"It's empty," she whispered, voice cracking slightly. "Silent, hollow, lifeless. When I open the door after a long day, it reverberates back at me. Nobody waits for me there. I sit alone at my table in a house that's beautiful and perfect but empty. There's no one to welcome me, no one who asks about my day or even notices if I come home late."

She blinked rapidly, fresh tears spilling down her cheeks. "You probably think that's ridiculous, that I'm selfish, ungrateful. But you can't imagine what it feels like, to have so much yet feel completely alone."

Ethan moved closer, carefully reaching out to place a gentle, reassuring hand on her arm, his touch grounding her. "I don't think you're ridiculous or selfish," he said softly, his voice soothing yet firm. "I think you're incredibly brave, and you've been alone for far too long."

She nodded weakly, gripping the water bottle tighter as if it were the only anchor holding her steady. She took a slow, shaky breath and continued softly, "And then these letters started arriving. At first, I was confused, even frightened. Who would write such things, these gentle, hopeful, comforting things, to someone like me? Initially, I thought it was a joke, some cruel prank from someone who wanted to mock the lonely, rich girl."

She shook her head slowly, a bitter smile curling briefly at the corner of her lips. "But the letters kept coming, and something strange happened, I started to look forward to them. For the first time in my life, someone seemed to see me, to notice the tiny details about who I really am beneath the image. They spoke as if they knew me intimately, knew exactly what to say to make me feel less alone."

She turned slowly toward Ethan, eyes wide and vulnerable, still shimmering from tears. "But then fear crept in again. Maybe these letters weren't kindness. Maybe they were a threat, a subtle warning from someone who wanted to harm me. Perhaps someone wanted to blackmail me or worse. I became paranoid, terrified. I needed to find out who this person was. That's why I came here, to uncover the mystery, to confront this anonymous writer who had unsettled my life."

Sophia's gaze was distant now, lost in memories and uncertainty. Ethan watched her closely, his pulse quickening slightly as he listened, his expression guarded yet deeply attentive.

"I suppose you must be wondering … " she spoke again, her voice barely more than a whisper now, ", why did I come specifically to Willow Creek to find this person." She hesitated, biting her lip nervously, struggling for the strength to reveal even this small truth. "It's because I used to live here, Ethan. A long time ago, when I was just a child."

Ethan's eyes gleamed briefly, something unreadable passing across his face, but Sophia was too caught up in her confession to notice. "I never thought I'd return," she continued quietly, her voice almost dreamlike. "But when those letters came, they mentioned things that only someone from here would know. And it made me realize that whoever was writing knew me from Willow Creek, knew me from before."

She inhaled softly, heart aching, eyes finally meeting his as if searching for something, recognition, understanding. "I was, "

", the only granddaughter of Mr. Carter," Ethan finished gently, softly completing her sentence, his voice steady and calm. "You lived at The Ridge."

Her heart froze, her breath catching painfully in her throat. Sophia stared at him, eyes wide with shock and disbelief. "How, " she stammered, confusion clouding her face, "how could you possibly know that?"

For a long moment, silence hung delicately between them, the truth now trembling on Ethan's lips. Sophia watched him, eyes wide and uncertain, feeling as though the ground beneath her had turned suddenly fragile. Ethan took a slow breath, steadying himself, his gaze gentle but intense, holding hers as if he was afraid, she might vanish if he looked away.

"I've always known you, Sophia," he began, his voice barely audible, carrying an earnestness that pierced straight through her heart. "Not just as the woman standing before me now but as someone from a past you might not even remember clearly."

She blinked, confusion gleaming in her eyes as she tilted her head, trying desperately to grasp at memories that lay stubbornly beyond reach. "What do you mean, Ethan? How could you possibly, ?"

He smiled softly, a gentle, nostalgic curve of his lips that softened the seriousness of his eyes. "My father was Nicholas Walker," he began gently, pausing carefully as he watched her expression shift subtly, recognition beginning to stir behind her confusion. "He was your father's closest friend. He had studied abroad, and when he came here, he brought a vision for change, for improvement, he wanted to help people. And your grandfather, Mr. Carter admired him deeply for that."

Sophia drew a shaky breath, the atmosphere choking around her, the fragments of a memory, faint and blurred, beginning to piece together within her mind. Her voice was faint, almost disbelieving, "Your father knew mine?"

Ethan nodded slowly, stepping closer, his voice gently encouraging as if guiding her back through mist-covered paths of the past. "They became friends quickly. My dad would visit The Ridge often, sometimes just to talk, sometimes to help your grandfather with his community projects. He brought me along occasionally. I was young, maybe thirteen or fourteen at most. You were barely seven, always shy, always quiet."

Sophia's breathing grew softer, shallower, as though she were afraid that a louder breath might scatter the delicate memories just beginning to form clearly. She listened intently, spellbound by the gentle cadence of Ethan's words, her heart aching quietly with each revealed detail.

"You rarely left The Ridge," Ethan continued, a tender smile forming slowly at the corners of his mouth. "You were always tucked away, watching us from a distance, as if too shy, or perhaps afraid to come close. But I remember one afternoon vividly. You finally stepped beyond the gates, following a cluster of butterflies into the orchard near the Ridge. You held a small woven basket in your tiny hands. I don't even think you noticed that I followed behind, making sure you wouldn't get lost."

Sophia's eyes softened slowly, tears shimmering faintly as she struggled to recall this fragile, long-forgotten scene. "Butterflies…" she murmured softly, almost inaudibly, as if the memory were gradually taking shape from the shadows in her mind.

Ethan smiled faintly, his gaze distant, his voice filled with gentle warmth. "Yes. You chased them with such innocence, laughter finally escaping your lips, your basket filling slowly with blossoms instead of butterflies.

You looked so free, so completely yourself. It was the first and only time I saw you so open, so unguarded. I remember thinking even then that I'd never seen anything so beautiful."

Sophia inhaled sharply, her heart trembling with an emotion she couldn't name, the memory slipping softly into clarity, a warm, golden afternoon, the laughter of her younger self, the soft murmur of wind through blooming branches.

"But then," Ethan's voice grew quieter, more hesitant now, shadowed with grief, "everything changed. Your father's death was the first tragic event that shattered that peace. My father, Nicholas Walker, was the one who delivered the news to your grandparents."

Sophia stiffened slightly, her breath hitching sharply, a flash of painful memory tightening her throat. Ethan stepped carefully closer, speaking softly, his voice gentle yet firm, guiding her through the past that still haunted them both.

"I was there that night, Sophia. I was fourteen, old enough to understand what had happened, to feel the deep sorrow of loss, but still young enough that my understanding was incomplete. You stood there, seven years old, clutching a worn bear in your small hands, your eyes wide with innocence and confusion. You didn't understand, not really, what you'd lost yet. But I did. I stood quietly in your shadow, hurting deeply for you, wishing somehow I could shield you from the pain I knew would come."

Sophia's tears spilled silently, her chest aching painfully with the burden of memories she had buried deeply beneath layers of adulthood, beneath the armor she had carefully crafted around her heart. Ethan reached gently, slowly, touching her hand as though afraid she might disappear again.

"After that, I came more often to The Ridge. Your grandfather was devastated, your grandmother brokenhearted, and you, you grew quieter each time. Every tragedy seemed to steal a piece of your voice, a fragment of your heart. You stopped laughing, stopped smiling. But even as your silence grew deeper, I saw you more clearly. I watched you, admired your strength, your courage. I always saw you, Sophia, even if you never saw me."

She stared up at him, eyes wide and vulnerable, tears cascading softly down her cheeks, overwhelmed by the quiet intensity of his confession. "Why didn't you ever tell me? Why did you keep this hidden all these days we've spent together?"

Ethan smiled faintly, his thumb brushing gently over the back of her hand. "Because I wanted you to find your own path back to the truth. I didn't want to burden you with memories you weren't ready to face yet. I wanted you to remember on your own terms, at your own pace. And maybe…maybe I was afraid, too. Afraid that reminding you of those days might push you away."

She shook her head softly, a quiet sob catching in her throat. "All these years, I thought nobody remembered, that I was forgotten, just a ghost left behind in Willow Creek."

He stepped even closer, gently pulling her into his warmth, arms circling protectively around her trembling form. "I could never forget, Sophia. I've conveyed those memories with me my whole life, waiting and hoping, never daring to believe you'd actually return."

She rested her forehead gently against his shoulder, the weight of everything she'd lost, everything she'd hidden, finally spilling free. "You've waited… all this time?"

He held her tighter, voice gentle but firm, whispering softly into her hair. "Always. You were my first real understanding of beauty, of courage, even in silence. Even when you were just a shy child chasing butterflies, I saw something in you that's stayed with me forever."

For a long moment, neither moved nor spoke. The stillness surrounding them was thick with vulnerability, the fragile revelations shared between them suspended like crystal threads, beautiful yet breakable. Sophia stared up at Ethan, her breathing soft and unsteady, the pulse of her heart loud in her ears. Ethan, steady yet cautious, watched her carefully, gauging each gleam of emotion that crossed her eyes.

Finally, he broke the silence with a voice as soft as the whispering wind through nearby leaves. "I always knew," he began gently, each word carefully chosen, "how deeply the rain frightened you. It wasn't hard to understand why. Every tragic moment in your life was marked by rain, storms coming to sweep away your happiness. Each time the clouds gathered, your heart braced for another loss."

Sophia felt her breath hitch, eyes widening as she took in the meaning behind his words, the realization striking her gently but firmly, like the first drops of an approaching storm.

Ethan continued quietly, his voice steady, gentle, never wavering. "I also knew about your hallucinations. I remember clearly the night you stood alone beneath that storm, sixteen years old, soaked and trembling outside your apartment in New York. You spoke to someone who wasn't there, your voice carrying words of loss and longing. I saw you, Sophia, I watched from a distance, my heart breaking with each word you whispered into the rain."

Her breath caught sharply, memories flooding back as she stared at him, shock and disbelief shining brightly in her eyes. "It was you?" she whispered, voice trembling with astonishment. "That night, on the street? The black bike, the stranger who saved me, it was you?"

He nodded gently, his gaze steady but soft, with quiet reassurance. "Yes. It was me. I couldn't interrupt at first, I knew you were in pain, trapped in some moment I couldn't see clearly. I wanted desperately to comfort you, to let you know you weren't alone. But I stayed back, watching carefully, until those street boys surrounded you. That was when I stepped in. I couldn't bear to see you frightened or harmed."

Sophia's eyes widened further, her heart pounding furiously, the revelation shaking her deeply. "All this time, " she breathed unsteadily, "you've been watching over me? Even then? But why, Ethan?"

He sighed softly, eyes heavy with emotion as he stepped closer, his voice gentle yet resolute. "Because, Sophia, you were never alone. You may have felt alone, believed you were abandoned, but you weren't. Your grandfather never stopped worrying about you. After your mother took you away, he was heartbroken. He couldn't protect you himself, couldn't shield you from the tragedies he knew would come. So he asked my father for help."

She shook her head slowly, tears shimmering, the world shifting quietly beneath her feet. "Your father, Nicholas Walker, he sent you to New York, too?"

Ethan nodded quietly, a gentle smile touching his lips. "Yes. Your grandfather arranged it all. My father explained everything to me, told me to keep a safe distance and never reveal myself to you, not until your studies were completed, not until you were strong enough to hear the truth. He knew that anything linked to Willow Creek would trigger painful memories, sending you back into your fight-or-flight instincts. Your grandfather wanted you safe, even if he couldn't do it himself."

Her chest tightened painfully, gratitude and disbelief washing through her in waves. "You've been protecting me... all these years?"

His smile softened further, eyes gentle and tender. "I was supposed to just watch over you, make sure nothing harmful touched your life. But Sophia, " he stepped closer still, his voice dropping to a gentle whisper, "how could I watch someone so strong, so brave, so beautifully resilient, and not feel something deeper? How could I not fall in love with someone who fought so silently, so gracefully, through storms she didn't deserve?"

She stood motionless, her heart thundering wildly, eyes fixed on him with quiet intensity, scarcely daring to breathe as he continued.

"I watched you walk home late at night, exhausted but determined, fighting your unseen battles. I saw how hard you worked, how you pushed yourself to your limits, building a world that you thought could never collapse around you. At first, I admired you from afar, respecting your space, hoping you'd eventually find peace, or perhaps even happiness again. But slowly, I began to lose hope. I saw your life fill with late nights, with lonely hours, with quiet despair disguised as success. I thought you had forgotten Willow Creek, forgotten the girl you once were."

Sophia swallowed tightly, her voice fragile and barely audible. "I thought I had, too," she whispered softly. "I tried to forget. To erase this place from my memories."

Ethan stepped gently closer, his gaze filled with profound understanding. "That's why I wrote the letters, Sophia. Because I saw you slipping away, deeper into that silence. I couldn't bear the thought of you forgetting the beauty of this place. Of forgetting there was once happiness, peace, and laughter here. I wanted to slowly replace your fear with warmth, to show you that beauty and hope still existed in Willow Creek. To remind you, gently, that somewhere in this world, someone was waiting patiently, quietly loving you from afar."

Sophia's breathing grew ragged, fresh tears spilling silently down her cheeks, her heart aching beautifully, painfully, with each whispered truth. She gazed up at Ethan, her eyes wide with disbelief, gratitude, and something deeper, something that felt frighteningly like love.

"All this time," she whispered unsteadily, her voice trembling with emotion, "you've been the one sending those letters. You've been the one watching, waiting, protecting me, all from the shadows. How could I never see it?"

Ethan reached gently, his fingertips softly brushing away her tears, his voice quiet yet firm. "You weren't supposed to, not until you were ready. But I couldn't let you remain forever in darkness. I wanted you to see that Willow Creek didn't only hold tragedy, it also held a heart that never stopped beating for you."

Sophia stepped forward slowly, reaching hesitantly, her fingers gently curling around his, her eyes searching his carefully, as if memorizing every detail of his face, every word spoken, every hidden truth finally unveiled. "Ethan, how could you love someone so broken?"

He smiled softly, leaning carefully toward her, their faces inches apart, his voice achingly gentle. "Because, Sophia Carter, your brokenness is your beauty. It's the strength you carry silently, the courage you show each day, the depth of your quiet resilience. Loving you was never a choice. It was something inevitable, something beyond my control."

Her lips parted slightly, breathing shallow as her eyes filled once more with tears, this time, tears of quiet joy, profound relief, and finally, understanding. She moved slowly into his embrace, resting her forehead gently against his chest, feeling his heartbeat steady, strong, grounding her.

He held her close, the silence enveloping them beautifully beneath the moonlit sky, beneath stars that shimmered gently like distant promises. Eventually, Sophia lifted her gaze, her voice a whisper filled with hope and vulnerability. "Will you stay, Ethan? Will you stay and help me learn to love Willow Creek again?"

He leaned closer, his gaze soft, filled with tender promise. "Always, Sophia. I've never left, not really. I'll stay as long as it takes for you to see this place again for what it truly is, not a place of tragedy, but one of healing, love, and endless possibility."

She smiled softly, her heart swelling with quiet joy, her voice gentle but certain. "Thank you, for everything, Ethan. For waiting, for protecting, for loving me when I didn't know I needed it."

He shook his head slowly, gently, smiling with profound tenderness. "Thank you, Sophia, for finally coming back. For finally seeing me."

She closed her eyes softly, breathing deeply, feeling a peace she'd never known settling gently into her heart.

He smiled warmly, gently, his eyes twinkling softly with gentle promise. "I'll tell you more, Sophia, every moment, every memory. But not tonight. Tonight, let's just be here, in this quiet, perfect moment."

Sophia exhaled softly, her heart finally, quietly, settling into a rhythm she'd been missing her entire life. "Until the rain falls again?" she whispered gently, the corners of her lips lifting into a hopeful smile.

Ethan leaned closer, his eyes holding hers gently, deeply, filled with promise and quiet love. "Until the rain falls again, Sophia. And then, I'll be here, holding your hand, reminding you that every storm eventually leads to something beautiful."

She smiled softly, closing her eyes, leaning gently into him beneath the starlit sky of Willow Creek, knowing deep within her heart that finally, beautifully, she had found her way home.

The End

www.ingramcontent.com/pod-product-compliance
Lightning Source LLC
Chambersburg PA
CBHW060537160726
47991CB00001B/364